Romantic Short Stories

SHARON KIZZIAH-HOLMES

Paperback Press Publishing

ISBN-10: 1491097236
ISBN-13: 978-1-4910972-3-6

DEDICATION

These stories are dedicated to my nephew and nieces. They inspired some of them, and there are more to come. I used their names, names of their children, friends and other family members. Though the names have been modified somewhat, those folks know who they are.

I love you all!

Aunt Sharon

ACKNOWLEDGMENTS

Thanks to my writing friends, in Ozarks Romance Authors and Sleuth's Ink Mystery Writers, for all of their support over the years.

A very special thanks to one of my BFF's and writing partner Kathleen Garnsey. I couldn't do this writing thing without her help and expertise.

To another BFF, Rhonda Austin, thank you for helping me plot some of my stories. You're the best! I appreciate your input.

Last but not least, thank you my husband, for your support over the years. You inspire my love stories.

THE RIDE OF A LIFETIME

"*O*kay, Whitley, I'll be by to pick you and Taylor up in an hour." Stacy Jones pushed the red 'OFF' button on her cell phone.

Why? Why did she have to be one of the three lucky ones to win a trip to a Texas dude ranch? She had better things to do this early in the spring. Smelly horses and tobacco-chewing cowboys were the last two things she wanted to waste time on. For a full week no less!

Her friends thought she'd make the perfect cowgirl. She'd dated cowboys before but they were drug store cowboys who'd never been on a horse in their lives. Neither had she for that matter, but she'd been known to ride a mechanical bull, and had to admit she was darned good at it. However, none of those relationships had worked and she had gotten past that faze of her life. If, or when, she started looking for the man of her dreams, he'd wear slacks and Polo shirts.

1

She thought about it for a moment and realized how prudish that was, but contrary to popular opinion, cowboys weren't the only men in Texas. Just because she was born and raised in Dallas, didn't mean she was destined to have a relationship with, or fall in love with, someone that wore boots, Wranglers, a silver belly hat and was associated with the word cow.

She took a deep breath. "Cowboys!" Exhaling, she headed back to her bedroom where a half-full suitcase awaited. There was nothing she could do about going on this trip. Her boss had all but insisted she and two of her co-workers, who also happened to be her best friends, take the time off to 'enjoy' themselves.

Stacy looked down at the small Yorkshire terrier that thrumped fast on her heels. "Sugarbear, what I'd really enjoy is staying right here at home with you. Maybe read a couple of good books watch some old movies and drink some wine." She reached down and stroked the terrier's tiny head. "But that's not going to happen."

"I only have one more thing to get." She went to the closet and pulled out the only cowboy boots she owned. "When I get home from this trip, Sugarbear, I'm going to throw these away. And don't ever let me buy another pair."

A small whine came from the dog's throat and Stacy smiled. Sometimes she thought the little thing really knew what she was saying.

She unzipped the flap on the pink canvas dog carrier she'd bought for Sugarbear a couple of years earlier. "Okay, girl, get in." The canine obeyed with a wagging tail. "If I have to endure a week with smelly old cowboys and horses, so do you."

Sure she had everything she needed; she gathered her things, walked out into the hallway of the apartment building, sat down her bag, then closed and locked her apartment door. "I guess we'd better go pick up Tay and Whitley, Sugar. Hopefully, they're looking forward to this escapade more than we are."

* * *

Stacy stopped her red Jeep Liberty just outside the entrance of the dude ranch. However, she didn't see anything that actually said 'Dude Ranch' on it. The big wrought iron archway held the initials THR. Out loud she read the nicely designed sign that was next to the entrance. "Tyler Horse Ranch. We give the best rides."

Tay laughed. "I wonder if that means the horseback rides," She raised her eyebrows. "Or the cowboy rides, if you know what I mean."

Cackling from the back seat Whitley added. "This may be more fun than we bargained for girls."

Both the other women's laughter was contagious and Stacy couldn't help but join in. She stepped on the gas and took the long dirt lane leading to a large log house. "You have to admit, it's beautiful out here."

Tay nodded. "Whoever owns this spread must have a bundle of money. Every inch of it has white rail fencing around it. And all these horses."

"Hence the name horse ranch, Tay."

"Don't be a smart ass, Stac."

"Yeah," Whitley added. "Those corrals are so neat and well kept. Look at that barn, it's huge."

Stacy studied the breath taking, loveliness of the rolling hills covered with green grass, Blue Bonnets and dotted with trees. The three large corrals held beautifully kept horses and some grazed on the hillside. At least they looked well kept. She'd never really been around to many of the animals before.

Out buildings that matched the log house were clean and well preserved. It took a lot of maintenance to keep a log home looking as perfect as this one. Unless it was fairly new, and she doubted that.

She began to relax. Maybe this wasn't going to be as bad as she'd first thought. It might be peaceful after all. Braking in front of the house, she put the Liberty in park. "We may as well get on with it girls. I'll let them know we're here."

When Stacy entered the big two story house, she couldn't believe the décor. She never dreamed she'd like such a masculine, rustic look, but she had to admit it was eye-catching.

A large round hooded fireplace stood in the middle of the room, surrounded by bulky southwestern style furniture. Not unlike things she'd seen before, but done with such taste it was inviting. She wondered what she'd expected. It wasn't this, that's for sure.

The ceiling stretched high above and the upstairs had the appearance of a loft with log railings surrounding it. Doors lined the walls and she knew behind them were guest rooms. The openness was refreshing.

"Howdy,"

She jumped at the sound of the deep voice behind her and quickly turned to meet the speaker. "He-hello." The simple word almost caught in her throat when she was greeted by the bright, warm smile of a tall good looking man. No, good looking wasn't the right description. The best looking man she'd ever seen, was.

He walked toward her with an outstretched hand. "You must be Whitley, from Neiman Marcus."

Accepting his handshake, she said, "Yes... ah, no, no, I'm sorry, I'm ah... Stacy. I work with Whitley." She took a deep breath and tried to still her pounding heart. What was wrong with her? The warmth of his touch lingered on her skin. His grip had been firm, yet gentle and his hand was so big it had almost engulfed hers.

"Nice to meet you."

She gazed into clear, sky blue eyes gently shaded by a grey Stetson. "Yes, it is." What? Yes it is? What a stupid thing to say. She felt like a babbling idiot and was thankful for the sound of the front door opening, the fumble of luggage and Sugarbear's bark.

Following the man's gaze, she glanced at her friends. She watched him walk toward the other women with the grace of a leopard. The heels of his cowboy boots thumped against the hard wood floor and matched the pulse beating in her temples. His shirt was neatly tucked into his tight fitting jeans and the name on his belt read Daron. Never had she seen Wranglers with a more perfect fit.

"What is that?" He pointed at the pink carrier.

She went over to the transporter, unzipped it and took her dog out. "This is my dog, Sugarbear."

"You call that a dog? Well, you'd better keep it close to you because that would be an appetizer for one of the real dogs we have around here."

He turned his attention to the other women. "Here, ladies, let me help you with those." He reached for the cases.

The smile in his eyes told Stacy Daron didn't mean the words he'd said about Sugar. She watched the muscles in his back flex as he picked the bags up and carried them down the hall.

"These two rooms on the right and that one on the left will be where you bunk for the week. I'll let y'all make the choice of who gets which room."

Stacy stood unmoving while her friends followed the hunk of a man down the hallway. She felt as if there was lead in her feet and couldn't force them move. Was she reverting back to her second childhood or to high school days when boys made her giddy? Damn her reaction to this man.

He put the suitcases down one by one next to each other. "Is this all y'all brought or do I need to get the rest?"

Whitley picked up two of the cases. "These are mine." She nodded toward the two remaining ones. "Those are Tay's, but Stacy's are still in the car."

"Okay. You ladies make yourselves at home. I'll get your friends luggage. Then you'll have just about enough time to get settled before suppers on the table."

When he approached Stacy he gestured one hand toward the door. "You lead the way Miss...?"

She had to get her heart rate under control. This was ridicules! "Jones. Stacy Jones. I don't think I caught your name." She was mildly aware of the attention her friends were paying to her conversation and not to getting settled in their rooms.

"Daron Tyler, ma'am, at your service."

Tay's voice was just above a whisper, but fully audible to Stacy.

"At your service, all right. You go girl."

Stacy vowed that when she got back inside, and out from under the scrutiny of Daron Tyler, she was going to kill her two co-worker/supposed friends.

Daron gestured toward the door. "Miss Jones, you'd better get that fur ball outside before it has an accident on the floor."

"You don't have to worry about that, Mr. Tyler. She's fully house broken." She turned on her heels. Maybe she was imagining it, but heat of his gaze burned into her back side as she walked out the door.

Daron smiled at the way Stacy Jones' long, dark brown hair swished on her back. The way the natural auburn highlights shone in the sunlight streaming through the skylights above brought out its warm beauty.

He especially admired how her perfectly shaped hind end swayed from side to side as she walked in front of him. The moment he saw her big brown eyes, he'd wanted to get to know the woman behind them, but it was his policy not to get involved with the guests and this time would be no different. He had to admit, though, he hadn't been intrigued by a woman this much in a long, long time.

She opened the back door of the Jeep Liberty and reached inside for a large suitcase. He took a place beside her. "Want me to get that?"

"I guess so," she replied taking a step back.

He was careful not to touch this beautiful creature. Their handshake a few minutes earlier sent shock waves up his arm. That was enough of a warning for him to keep his distance even if he didn't have a policy. However, now the soft scent of honeysuckle wafted from her hair into his nostrils. Hoping the breath he drew wasn't too obvious; he held it and savored the aroma.

It wasn't often a woman captured his attention, but she was different. Being near her made him quiver inside. The winter months at the ranch had been long and lonely, but every year had been the same. Why had meeting the first guest of this season affected him this way? It would pass. It had to.

He led the way back into the house and down the hallway. "It looks like your friends chose the two rooms on the left. Guess they didn't look in here." He opened the door and entered his favorite guest room in the house.

"This is the only guest suite we have." He set the baggage down and glanced around the large room.

"This is the parlor. Besides the master suite, it's the only room with its own fireplace. Your bedroom and bathroom are through that door."

She looked in the direction he pointed. "Thank you, Mr. Tyler. I must say, I'm glad my friends didn't look in here. It's beautiful. And the décor, may I ask who did it for you?"

"I did."

"And the house?"

"Yep."

"Really?"

The surprise in her voice made him laugh. "Is that so unbelievable?"

"Well, no, but I never thought... ah... well..."

"That a cowboy could have good taste? I hear it all the time, so don't feel bad." He stepped away, but kept looking at Stacy. What he really wanted to do was brush her beautiful blushing cheek with the back of his hand.

"Supper'll be on the table in an hour." He walked to the door, then turned back to face the most captivating woman he'd ever met. "Oh, and please, call me Daron." He went through the doorway and closed the door behind him only to notice the other two women stood there watching. He tipped his hat to them. "Ladies."

They giggled as he walked down the hall and out of their sight. He didn't care what they thought of him, but he wished he knew what Miss Jones was thinking.

Rounding the corner into the kitchen, wonderful aromas of roast beef, potatoes and freshly baked pies greeted him. His head cook and bottle washer Lupe, a short, round Mexican woman with her graying black hair piled in a bun atop her head, stood at the stove.

"Did you get them all settled, son." The older woman put butter into the mashed potatoes and began to stir them.

"Yep." He leaned against the kitchen counter and made a mock effort to stick his finger in the potatoes. He knew he'd get slapped and her small brown hand barely missed him.

"You stop that. This is for the guests."

One of his favorite things was Lupe's Mexican accent. She and her husband Manuel had been his life savers after his folks passed. "You mean I don't get any?"

"You know exactly what I mean. Now go wash up."

He reached again, but this time he hit his mark. Running toward the stairs, he put the potatoes in his mouth and smiled as Lupe sent a verbal protest to him in Spanish, knowing he didn't understand a word.

The hot water from the shower beat down on his chest while his thoughts wandered to the bathroom in the suite below his. He closed his eyes and imagined Stacy Jones with drops of water glistening on her naked, ivory skin.

Stacy studied herself in the mirror. She'd put on her best pair of designer jeans and a short sleeved white blouse that showed just enough cleavage. Why she was going all out just to go to supper she didn't know. She was in the country at a horse ranch for gosh sakes, but something made her want to look her best. Who was she fooling? She knew exactly why she wanted to look good and his name was Daron Tyler.

The knock at the door pulled her from her self-evaluation. "Just a minute." She put on her earrings as she went to the door, when she got there, she reached for the knob and opened it. Whitley and Tay rushed into the room.

"Wow, this is really nice," Tay said. "I wish I'd have gotten this room."

"Yeah, me too." Whitley ran her hand across the rough wood mantle of the fireplace.

"You should have been paying more attention to the rooms instead of to what I was doing, so, ha ha, too late. It's mine."

Tay plopped down on the sofa. "I think that good looking cowboy's yours, too. And look at you, you're glowing."

Stacy furrowed her brow. "What are you talking about?"

"We saw the way he looked at you, with that little gleam in those, beautiful blue eyes. I think you saw it too."

She felt a flush rush to her cheeks. At least they didn't notice how she was a babbling fool in front of him. "I did not! You must have been imagining things. But I heard what you said earlier in the hallway. I wish you wouldn't do things like that. He might have heard you, too."

"Well, I know one thing for sure, if you don't take him, Stac, I'm going to. Mrs. Taylor Tyler. How does it sound?"

Tay stood and ran her fingers through her medium length red curls. For an instant, jealousy stilled Stacy's heart and blood boiled in her veins. What was she thinking? She'd just met the guy and had no say over what he or her friend did. She closed her eyes and took a moment to let the feeling go.

Whitley opened the door leading to the hallway. "It sounds goofy, either way, it seems Daron Tyler is taken. I can't wait to see the rest of the cowpokes around here."

"You girls do what you want," Stacy said. "But look out, I know about those cowboys and I intend to keep my distance."

She hoped those intentions weren't more than she could ask of herself. No, she had to keep her distance. Her heart depended on it.

CHAPTER 2

Stacy leaned her head back and enjoyed the warmth of the morning sun on her face. The walk to the barn would have been peaceful if she was alone, but her friends were being flirtatious and obnoxious toward Daron. She was probably too hard on them, but it seemed they were doing their best to embarrass her.

Spiced men's cologne flowed in the wake of their host as she walked behind him into the barn. She'd noticed at the supper table the night before that he didn't smell at all like sweat, tobacco and beer. And today she was even more aware of his clean, manly scent. She only wished he did reek then maybe she wouldn't be so attracted to him.

The barn was huge with a roomy hay covered loft above. The ground floor held many stalls, tack hung neatly on the walls along with various tools she didn't recognize. Fresh straw lay on the floor under all of the horse's feet and each horse was groomed to perfection.

Whitley walked up beside her. "It doesn't stink in here like I expected."

"No it doesn't," she replied. The smell of leather, straw, oats and whatever else was supposed to be in a barn, were actually pleasant.

"Look over there." Whitley pointed in the direction of an open area where four cowboys stood. "Three of those guys are about our age, and the other is Lupe's hubby. Just call me Dale Evans because one of the three of those guys is going to be my Roy Rogers."

Stacy laughed and shook her head. She'd always loved Whitley's since of humor. "Girl, we didn't come here to get boyfriends, we came to have a relaxing week at a dude ranch. Are men all you and Tay ever think about?" Stacy didn't know why she asked that question, she already knew the answer. "Never mind."

Daron took something out of a sack next to one of the stalls. "Stacy, this is Samantha, we call her Sammy. She'll be your mount for the next few days."

The sound of his voice saying her name, sent shivers up her spine. She took a carrot from his hand careful not to touch his fingers.

"Give her that and she'll love you forever. Or at least until you leave on Sunday." He turned and motioned the others toward the east end of the barn.

His light hearted chuckle touched her heart. She gave Sammy the vegetable and watched as Daron introduced Whitley and Tay to their mounts. The look on the handsome man's face said he was proud of his place and loved each and every animal. She admired that.

Daron lifted his hand and waved to the men in the open area. "Hey, Brian, Joe Ray, would you come help these ladies learn how to bridle and saddle their horses, please?"

"Sure thing, D-man." One of them replied as they fulfilled his request.

"And, Hal, would you go inside and make sure Lupe sees to it that, that little ankle biter of Miss. Jones' doesn't get out and get under foot. Or get eaten by one of the Labs or Heelers?"

"I'm on it, D."

When Daron turned in her direction her knees threatened to buckle beneath her. His long strides were relaxed but powerful at the same time.

How could that be? A handshake that was firm yet gentle, strides that were relaxed yet powerful… it seemed this man was the epitome of oxymoron's. Maybe it was all in her mind but she knew one thing. He was getting closer and the butterflies in her stomach refused to be still.

"You ready to learn about saddling a horse?" He asked opening the stall gate.

She swallowed hard and fought to keep her voice steady. "If I have to."

He walked into the stall ahead of her and handed her a bridle. "What's that mean? Didn't you want to come to THR?"

"Not exactly. We all three won this trip at our company Christmas party. It wasn't so much that we won it. I think our boss actually gave us the trip, so we were kind of forced into it. What are the odds that three best friends would win a trip all at the same time."

"Oh, I see." He helped her place the bridle on Sammy's head and showed her how to fasten the straps. "What was the motive?"

"I really don't know except our job is very stressful.

"You might as well make the best of it then, and try to enjoy the ranch."

"I thought this place would be more, I don't know, like the dude ranches you see in the old westerns."

"Dude ranch? We're anything but a dude ranch, Miss Jones. We are a fully functioning horse ranch. We entertain a few guests each year, teach them how to ride, rope if they want but mainly to relax and enjoy life. Something you folks from the city rarely do."

"Please, call me Stacy. By the way, how would you know what we do in the city?"

He handed her the saddle blanket. "I lived in L.A. for a few years. It's not that much different than Dallas. Except there ain't many cowboys."

She started to place the blanket on Sammy's back, but a touch of his hand on her arm stopped her.

"You should always show your mount the blanket and the saddle before you put it on their back. That way they will know what's coming."

"That's understandable." She put the blanket where Sammy could see it than proceeded to place it on her back. "So, what did you do in L.A.?"

He gave her little help lifting the saddle, but

was sure it didn't fall. "Oh, it doesn't matter. I don't do that anymore."

"No, really, I'd like to know." As she studied his face and saw the small scar across the bridge of his nose and another that ran along his jaw line, she found herself wanting to know everything about him.

"Sammy, you stop that," he said as he tightened the saddle strap under the mare's belly.

The poor horse wasn't moving. "What's she doing?"

"Puffing out her belly so I can't get this strap tightened. It's an old trick and if you're not aware of it you can be on your butt on the ground almost as soon as you try to mount."

She petted the horses behind. "Sammy you're a sneaky girl."

"Ever rode a horse before?"

"No, but I'm sure I can."

"How can you be so sure?"

"I won the woman's mechanical bull competition two years in a row at The Bigger 'n' Dallas club. Of course, that was a few years back, but I bet I can still do it."

"Let's hope so. Here." He handed her the reins. "We're fallin' behind, everyone else is already outside."

They were alone in the barn and their closeness suddenly became awkward. She was aware of the warmth of his body standing next to her. When she looked up she met his gaze and again her knees wanted to give way. Seconds seemed like minutes.

She couldn't look away, his eyes were

mesmerizing. The lump in her throat went down hard and her breath caught when she tried to speak. "W-we'd better go then."

Slowly his face came closer to hers, his breath like a warm, gentle breeze on her lips. She forced air into her lungs while anticipation threatened to make her swoon. Oh, he was going to kiss her.

"Hey, come on y'all. We have some riding to do."

Daron turned away from her as quickly as she did from him. They were acting like a couple of kids caught with their hands in the cookie jar and she felt guilty for nothing.

Tay shrugged her shoulders. "Oooh, bad timing. Sorry."

"No, you're okay." Daron replied, walking out of the stall. "We were just…just about to…come outside."

* * *

The night was cool, but not cold. Daron stoked the fire he'd built in the pit behind the house. Trees surrounded the area and hay bales were placed around the pit. This was a place where he and the hands gathered after a day's work to unwind.

Brian approached with his guitar, Hal with his harmonica and Manual with his open top Mexican bass. Daron had placed his guitar against one of the bales before he fired up the wood. Joe Ray didn't play, but he was the best singer of them all, however, they all took their turn.

The music his friends made behind him faded

into the background of his thoughts. How could he have let it happen? He was so close to kissing her. Closer than he'd come to kissing a woman in a long time.

Something had come over him he couldn't explain, but he'd be damned if he'd let it happen again. That was easier said than done. Stacy Jones was playing havoc with his emotions and he didn't even know the woman. It had to be physical attraction, nothing else. It had been so long since he'd... No, he was attracted to her, but this feeling was more than that.

The strings of his heart pulled tighter every time he looked at her. When he was close to her, it was worse. Falling in love was something he didn't want in his life right now. The ranch was doing better than it had in years and he didn't need a woman trying to pull him away from all he'd worked for. Love, why did he even think of that?

"Daron, I'm talking to you. Are you okay?" Lupe put her arm around his waist.

"Sorry, Lupita. Just thinking." Her knowing smile told him she was aware of his thoughts.

"She is beautiful, isn't she?"

"Who?"

"Don't you act like you don't know who I'm talking about, young man, Miss. Jones, that's who."

"Oh, yes, they're all beautiful."

"Her eyes sparkle when she looks at you and her cheeks flushed when you talk."

"It must be the wine she had a supper."

"Trying to fool this old lady? Well, don't, I've known you almost all of your twenty nine years and

I can see behind those lying eyes of yours. You're just as interested in her. But don't forget, she's a guest and you know the policy. You made it."

The older woman's concern warmed him. For the five years he was gone from the ranch, she and Manuel had done all they could to keep it up, but when Manny had his heart attack, Daron knew it was time to come home. He loved both of them with all of his heart, and was thankful for what they'd done for him.

He put his arm around Lupe's shoulder. "Okay, okay, I get your drift. I'll do my best."

She flashed him a knowing look. "Humph!" she said and walked away. Looking back in his direction she called out, "You only have a few days left. You can do it."

Hopefully she was right, but he was afraid his heart would fight him every step of the way. He knew it would, because his chest tightened at that very moment, as Stacy walked out the back door and started toward him.

Her gaze was averted as if she were trying not to look him in the eye. That's the way it had been all day. His heart sank. Maybe she didn't like him. Maybe Lupe was wrong about what she'd said. What the hell did it matter anyway? He knew what he had to do.

* * *

"Come here, Sugarbear." Stacy sat on the sofa studying the yellow, blue and orange flames as they flickered in the fireplace. "You're my favorite little cuddle bunny. You know that?" The terrier jumped up, took her place beside her master, turned in circles then finely curled into a ball and lay down.

Stroking the dogs head and knowing she'd have to answer her questions in her own mind, she asked anyway. "What do you think of Mr. Daron Tyler, Sugar?"

Every time Daron was in the room, Sugarbear made a b-line right to him. He would lovingly pick her up and say his hello's then go on about his business. Sugarbear loved him already, Stacy knew that.

As for herself, she wasn't sure what was in her heart, or her mind. She'd had boyfriends before, but none that made her feel like he did. None that had touched the part of her heart Daron did. Merely hearing his voice made her pulse race. She had tried like hell to stop the feelings as soon as they surfaced, but it was harder than she'd ever imagined.

In some way, she was thankful that he had appointed Hal her official 'guide' or whatever you might call it, and Daron just ramrod' from a distance. She had to admit the time she'd spent at the ranch was relaxing. No pressure from any direction, no phone calls and no tension, especially if Daron wasn't around and there was only tension then because of her feelings for him.

Feelings? How could she have feelings for someone she'd just met? That was a question she'd asked herself every day since she'd arrived.

It baffled her more than it did Tay and Whitley, who thought she was crazy for not going after him.

However, she knew by the distance he had put between him and herself, that he didn't want anything to do with her.

That was just fine. In a couple of days she'd be leaving. She would put more than a hundred miles between them, and all of this behind her.

Forgetting someone, who could very well be the man of her dreams, might be hard, but she'd manage. She'd gotten over relationships before, so this would be easy because she and Daron didn't have a relationship.

A near kiss couldn't be called a liaison by any means, but every night she dreamt of what that kiss would have been like. How his lips would have felt pressed against hers.

She stood, then closed the glass doors of the fireplace. It was early, but she was ready to turn in. "Let's go to bed, Sugarbear, I've got a lot to do in the morning to get ready for the ride." She didn't know exactly what kind of ride they would be on tomorrow. The hands had kept it from them, but she knew it would be something different and exciting.

She actually enjoyed the time she spent with the horses. Grooming Samantha after a ride was as relaxing for her as it was for Sammy.

The openness of the outdoors was so much different than her cubical of an office at Neiman. Being a buyer was one thing she'd enjoyed more than most anything she'd ever done, but being a cowgirl ran a close second.

No, she didn't just think that, did she? Yes, she did. As much as being a cowgirl went against her former beliefs, it was true. With or without Daron

Tyler, she could make a life of living on a ranch. However, having him around would be a dream come true.

She turned off the bedside lamp then snuggled under the covers. Smiling, she wondered if Daron's kiss would be an oxymoron like his handshake and the way he walked.

Would his lips be hard and at the same time soft? Would he be wildly passionate, yet caring? "Damnit, Sugar, why do I do this to myself every night?" she asked turning over in the bed. "I need a good book to get my mind off that man."

She knew a book wouldn't do the trick. Only getting away from here… no, getting away from Daron would be the only thing to suppress her wanting.

CHAPTER 3

"*H*ead 'em up, move 'em out!" Daron slapped a rope against his leg. The noise would get the cattle moving. "Woo doggie, get up!"

Dust sifted up from the ground as the herd started to stir. He hadn't told Stacy and the other girls they'd be on a cattle drive today and by the look on Tay and Whitley's faces, they didn't like it much.

On the other hand, Stacy seemed to take to it like a duck to water. He wondered how she'd feel if she knew it was going to take hours to complete the drive and get back to the ranch.

She amazed him in more ways than one. It didn't matter what task she'd been given on the ranch, she jumped right in and wasn't afraid to get her hands dirty. She shoveled manure without a gripe, forked hay into the stalls, fed the animals and on top of all that, insisted on helping Lupita in the kitchen. And now he learned she could whistle like a grown man at the herd, but she was all woman.

Even with her hair pulled into a ponytail at the

nape of her neck and wearing a wrinkled old cowboy hat she'd borrowed from Hal, she was beautiful.

She looked as if she'd been riding all of her life. Her long legs hugged Sammy's belly while her bottom fit perfectly in the saddle.

No matter how hard he'd tried, he couldn't stop himself from imagining what it would be like to run his hands up the soft skin of her legs and cup her bottom in his palms. No one would ever know the torture he'd put himself through trying to keep space between him, and that fine-looking woman.

He had never taken his meals away from the guests, but this week he'd felt it necessary. Lupe had warned him and he took her advice to heart. Stacy Jones was one woman he could easily fall in love with.

In his years in L.A. he'd had the reputation of being a womanizer. That was okay with him, but in truth he hadn't been intimate with many women in his lifetime. There had never been anyone who had really tripped his trigger until now. His high school sweetheart came the closest, but when she left for college, it was out of sight out of mind for him.

He had a feeling it was going to be different when Miss Jones left the ranch. How long would he dream of her. How long would he crave to hold her in his arms, kiss her lips and make love to her in the early morning hours?

He glanced up to see a young calf beginning to stray. "Hal, help Tay keep those calves in with the herd!" Hal was a good man. One of the best he'd ever had work for him. Daron knew he didn't have to tell the man how to do his job, but he was trying to get his mind off Stacy.

It was virtually impossible. Hell, she was less than one hundred feet away from him looking gorgeous atop Samantha's back. The sound of horses' hooves galloped up beside him.

"Penny for your thoughts." Whitley pushed a strand of hair from her face.

She and Tay had been doing their damndest to sabotage his efforts of staying away from their friend.

"The only thing I'm thinking of, Miss Whitley, is getting this herd to their destination." He wondered if she knew he was lying.

"Oh, really. Is that why you keep staring at Stacy?"

Was it that obvious? "You must be mistaken. I'm keeping an eye on everyone."

"Yeah, right. Why don't you just admit there are sparks between you two and discard that silly old rule of yours not to get involved with your 'guests'? Stacy's a great gal, really."

"Miss Whitley, how I run my business is my business. My love life is also my business and I'd thank you for keeping out of it." He hadn't meant to sound so harsh, but damnit, he was having a hard enough time on his own trying to keep from falling in love with the woman. The last thing he needed was this.

The smile that crossed the young ladies face was bright. He was sure she hadn't heard what he'd said or she'd have gotten her feelings hurt or some other girlie thing. At least he hoped she'd take the hint.

Whitley's laughter penetrated the air. "Oh, Mr. Tyler, you are one man I can see right through."

When he looked into Whitley's face, he saw seriousness come to her eyes as their gaze met. "I've known Stacy for a long time. She hasn't had too many boyfriends over the years and definitely not many lovers. She's been waiting for the right one to come along like a good woman should. I know my friend Mr. Tyler, she'd in love."

He couldn't speak. The look on Whitley's face told him she really cared for Stacy. Maybe it was true. Maybe he was foolish for not following his heart.

"Don't let her go, Daron. Don't wait until we leave and realize you've made the biggest mistake of your life. You might lose the best thing that could ever happen to you."

* * *

Dusk was just beyond the horizon. Every bone in Stacy's body ached. Herding cattle on horseback was one thing that had never crossed her mind. As unnatural as this would have been a week ago, she'd had a great time. However, she looked forward to getting back to the ranch so she could take a long hot bath. One of Lupe's good meals would hit the spot, too.

She had come to admire the older woman and took pleasure in her company. It was amazing, at her age, how she achieved her daily tasks. The woman's niece was the housekeeper that took care of cleaning the guestrooms and other household chores. Lupe mainly did the cooking for the guests and the hands. That in itself was a full time job.

Manuel helped with light chores, but Stacy was surprised to find out that Daron actually did most of the work around the ranch. That explained how he stayed in such good physical condition.

She inhaled, stretched as well as she could in the saddle and exhaled the long breath. The house, visible in the distance, was inviting. She couldn't wait to get there.

"Hey."

"Damn!" she said, when startled by Tay's voice beside her.

"What are you daydreaming about? Daron Tyler."

"Tay, you know what? You and Whitley need to get off my back about him. I don't want anything to do with the man, and it's clear he feels the same way."

"Are you nuts? He wants everything to do with you. You can tell by the way he steel's glances at you when he thinks no one is looking."

"Oh, really? I haven't noticed."

"Maybe that's because you do the same thing. You know, none of us are blind. You two need to talk."

"What would you have me say to him? Hey, Daron, Tay said you've been looking at me, what's the deal?"

"Don't be stupid. You know what I mean."

"No, don't you be stupid. There's nothing between me and Daron Tyler and never will be.

Now, can we change the subject? Please?"

"Okay, whatever."

The short silence between them brought the ride closer to the end of the trail. Maybe they'd get to the house and she could lock herself in her room for the evening. She new better than that. The cowboy music the guys played each night around the fire was her favorite part of the day. She'd probably never have the experience again, so she didn't want to miss it.

Whitley rode up beside her and Tay. "Hey, Brian just said there's a barn dance tomorrow night. You guys want to go?"

Tay smiled. "I've never been to a Saturday night barn dance, have you, Stac?"

"No."

"Want to go?"

Her first reaction was to say no, but why? What could it hurt? It might even be fun. "Sure. Will they have beer?"

"Are you kidding?" Whitley laughed. "Do you know of any dance in the state of Texas where there's no beer?"

She chuckled. "I guess that was a dumb question. Well, who wants to be designated driver?"

Whitley reined her horse through the back gate leading onto the property. "We won't need one; it's going to be in the THR barn. And guess what? I'm going to the dance with Brian."

"Brian?" Tay asked. "How'd you manage that?"

"What do you mean, how did I manage it? I asked him."

One thing Stacy could say about her friend Whitley is she wasn't at all shy. She joined her friends in laughter, which was hard not to do. As she always noticed, their laughter was contagious.

Behind the good heartedness, she felt a pang of regret. The morning after the dance would mean they had to leave. Something she wasn't looking forward to. She would miss her afternoon strolls in the foothills, and the flat out leisure time of vacation. The evening sing along, and most of all, seeing Daron's face every day.

Oh, well, it was something she'd have to deal with. Now that she thought about it, the sooner the better. Life would be back to normal at the first of the week and she'd be glad for it.

* * *

"Yeeee Hawwww!" Joe Ray yelled into the microphone from the makeshift stage in the corner of the barn. "Grab your partner and doe-see-doe."

Daron strummed his electric guitar to the beat of the music. The square dancers looked like they were having a great time. He enjoyed seeing the smile on Stacy's face as she joined in the dance.

He liked people watching, and what better place to do it from than the band-stand. Brian had kept most of his attention on Miss Whitley since she'd arrived witch was okay with him, because his policy was his own. He didn't put any restrictions on the hands except they be gentlemanly in all that they do when it comes to guests. It was hard for Brian to dance with her when he was playing, but he'd managed to slip a couple of two steps in.

Hal and Tay had become pretty close friends, but he hadn't seen any love interest there, however they had danced together when Hal wasn't playing his harmonica with the band.

It hadn't gone unnoticed that every available man in the place had danced with Stacy. She was the prettiest girl there and her smile lit up the room. Hell, her smile lit up his heart like no other.

He was thankful the girls had been the only visitors at the ranch the past week. It made for a more personal experience and he hoped they'd all enjoyed it. He knew he had, even though he hadn't been as much a part of it as usual. But he'd made his decision to keep his distance and had done a damn good job of it.

That's why he didn't think one dance with Stacy tonight would hurt. She was a hell of a good dancer and he was going to ask her on the next slow song he wasn't playing on. He just wanted to hold her one time before she left the next morning. This would be his only chance to see if she fit in his arms as well as he'd imagined she would.

Joe Ray made the announcement, "This will be the last song of the night folks."

Hal pulled out his harmonica and began to blow a soft slow song. Last song? Time had gone by faster than Daron had thought possible. Now was his only opportunity to hold the most beautiful woman he'd ever known.

He put his guitar aside and stepped down to the dance floor. The lights were turned off for the last song allowing the dime flames of the lanterns that burned on the railings to offer a soft glow. He glanced around for Stacy, but in the matter of an instant she had disappeared. Where could she have gone?

Then he spotted her in another man's arms. Fire shot through his heart. He'd be damned if he'd let one more cowboy steel his chance to hold her.

When he approached the two as they swayed on the dance floor, he caught Stacy watching his every movement. He didn't look away this time, he focused on her beautiful brown eyes and the way the dim glow of the oil lamps made them sparkle.

After Daron tapped him on the shoulder, without a word, the man walked away and stacy held his gaze as she slipped into his arms. He took the lead and it felt right, perfect just as he knew it would, when she gently laid her head on against him.

There it was again, the sweet fragrance of honeysuckle. The strings of his heart felt like a lasso as they tightened their hold. Every muscle of his body was aware of how natural it felt when she relaxed into his embrace. It was a moment he didn't want to end.

This was a memory Stacy would burn into her mind so she could close her eyes and see it for a life time. Being in Daron's arms was more natural than anything she'd ever felt. She wanted to savor the essence of his smell, his touch, the way his arms felt around her... him.

For the last few days, she'd fought the feelings in her heart. She would fight them once again, but not now. Not while he held her like he had in her dreams.

She could get used to being close to this man. His body was warm and she felt safe when in his embrace. She longed to tell him the bundle of emotions that flowed through her heart, her mind, but she dare not. She didn't want to do anything to end this moment.

It didn't matter if there were people all around them. To her they waltzed in their own little world. A world she wished could belong to her forever and not for just one dance.

Soon, Joe Ray's voice pulled her back to reality, but the song wasn't over and she couldn't bring herself to lift her head from Daron's strong chest.

"Good night, folks, we hope you had a good time. Please be careful going home and enjoy the rest of, the last dance."

She tilted her head upward to look into Daron's blue eyes once again. His gaze threatened to take her breath as they continued to sway to the music. Momentarily, he released his embrace, only to pull off his Stetson and place it in his hand against her back. He ran his fingers through his untidy blond hair, then placed his other hand behind her back as well.

The gesture forced her, without protest, to place both arms around his neck. Her fingers entwined with his soft, golden locks only moments before the music ended. The world around them, her world, stopped when he bent and place the tiniest whisper of a kiss on her lips.

"Thank you."

His warm breath brushed her ear causing a shiver to course through her body. His words were barely audible, his voice, husky. She wanted him. More than anything, she wanted him, but the moment was over.

The lights came up, the band played a quick little diddy, said goodnight and started packing up.

Reluctantly, she dropped her arms. "No, thank you, for showing us such a great time at the ranch." She could tell he was pressed for words and what she had felt was so natural only moments ago, now seemed awkward.

She smiled up at him. "You'd better go and get your guitar." The look he gave her smoldered and heated her to the very core, but his words chilled her to the bone.

"You're right. I'd better go." He placed his hat back on his head and in the blink of an eye, he turned and walked away.

Had he experienced the same feelings she had for those few short minutes or had it all been a game to him? One he'd played in the past with other women guests?

She didn't know and didn't care. That was her moment and she would relish in it always.

CHAPTER 4

*S*tacy walked back to the house alone, ate a snack with Lupe and Manuel then went to bed. She heard the back door of the house open then close. It was Daron because Sugarbear sniffed under her bedroom door and began to whine. She wanted out so she could go and greet him.

He was so close yet so far away. His room was just above hers and not long after he arrived home she heard the shower water running. What was in his head? Did he think of her, remember their dance the way she did?

She closed her lids and reflected on the short time she'd spent in his arms. It went over in her mind at least a hundred times. As it would, she was sure, for many nights to come.

When she opened her eyes, she realized she'd been asleep only a few hours, but it was impossible for her to drift off again. She was wide awake.

After she dressed she went out to the back of

the house and sat on one of the hay bales by the fire pit. The morning sun threatened to peek over the foothills that surrounded Tyler Horse Ranch. She had never seen anything more beautiful, unless of course it was, Daron Tyler.

Today she would leave and all of this would be only a memory. She stood and walked toward the barn wondering if Sammy would be up for a ride this early. Watching the sunrise from atop one of the hills surly would be a highlight of her stay here.

Now that she felt comfortable with riding she had no fear of going out by herself. The fresh, crisp morning air would help her clear her mind, and get ready to make the trip back to Dallas.

She opened the barn door and inhaled its aromas. Ones she'd grown accustom to in the past week. Ones she'd grown to love.

When she approached Samantha's stall it was almost like the mare had been waiting for her. "Good morning, girl."

Sammy bobbed her head up and down then neighed her greeting. She was a beautiful horse and held a special spot in Stacy's heart. "How would you like to go out and watch the sunrise?"

Again, the mare bobbed her head.

"Okay, then, let's do it."

After showing the horse blanket to Sammy, Stacy placed it on her back. She remembered how heavy the saddle was the first time she lifted it. Even if she'd only boosted onto the horses back six or seven times before, now it seemed like second nature.

She honestly wondered if riding the mechanical

bull had helped her take to real riding better. Thankful the party life she'd led a couple of years ago was behind her, she was still grateful for some of the things she'd learned from it.

Unfortunately, she thought she'd been taught not to give her heart to a cowboy, but apparently that lesson went in one ear and out the other.

She pulled the belly strap on the saddle as tight as she could get it. Most of the time Joe Ray was there to heave it tighter, but Sammy wasn't playing the pooch-her-belly-out trick today.

"You know Sam, I think you like me just about as much as I like you. I only wished the same went for your master."

Sammy pawed the ground and made her laugh. "You can understand me just like Sugarbear, can't you? I never knew horses were so smart."

With the reins, she led Sammy into the main breezeway of the barn then out into the open. Once she mounted, she headed to the foothills and the almost peaking sunrise.

"Oh, isn't it beautiful, Sam?" she said patting the horses neck from the saddle. "It's everything I imagined and more." She chuckled at the flutter of her heart when she thought of Daron.

"Girl, did you know I think I'm in love with your Mr. Tyler? Well, I do. I just hope I can forget about him when I get back to Dallas and real life."

This had been a fairy tale week for her, except for avoiding Daron, she had been happier this week than she could ever remember. Maybe it was because she could watch him from a distance. Maybe because she knew he was nearby and if she really needed him, he would be there.

Whatever it was she was glad for it and would cherish the memories forever. "Let's ride a little longer, what do you say? I want to savor everything about this trip before I have to go home. I may never get the chance again."

She pressed her heels into the mare's side, but something was wrong. Sammy wouldn't budge. She nudged her again. "Come on, girl, let's go."

* * *

Everyone was at the breakfast table but Stacy. Daron wondered if she was going to sleep all day. Sleep was something he got little of the night before. The warmth of Stacy's body in his embrace haunted him. How could anything feel so right in such a short time?

Whatever. He wouldn't have to worry about it much longer. In a few hours she'd be gone and they would get ready for their next round of guests. However, he was sure her memory would taunt his nights, his dreams. How stupid was that?

"I think I hear Sugarbear scratching at the door from inside Stacy's bedroom. That girl is sleeping heavy this morning," Tay said.

"Must have been that last dance that wore her down," Whitley taunted.

Daron met Whitley's more than amused gaze and shot her, what he hoped was, a warning glance. Then he heard Sugarbear cry and scratch once again. "Why don't one of you go and let that ankle biter out before she peels the finish off the door."

"Why don't you go let her out, it's your house," Tay chided.

What was he scared of? Steeling a glance into Stacy's room? "Okay."

He made his way down the hallway and to her door. The lump in his throat went down hard when he reached for the knob. Sugar was more frantic than ever, but it seemed it was more distant then the main door.

Why was his heart beating so hard, so fast? He knew the answer but tried to ignore it as he opened the door. Stacy's unique honeysuckle sent drifted from the room into the air in the hallway. Sugarbear wasn't inside that door, but she was scratching from inside Stacy's bedroom door.

If Stacy woke up while he had her door open, what would she think he was doing? Being perverted and watching her in her slumber? Or would she think he was trying to catch a glimpse of her tanned bare skin against the white of the sheets? He didn't care. He was here now and all he intended to do was let the dog out.

He slowly opened the gateway to Stacy's bedroom. Sugarbear ran out, barked and jumped up on his leg. Before his attention went to the terrier, he stole a glance into the room.

The light was dim, but it was clear Stacy wasn't there. He studied the empty space. Her bags weren't packed, the clothes she'd worn to the dance lay neatly over the back of a chair and her purse sat open on the bed.

He entered the kitchen again. "Has anyone seen Stacy this morning?"

Just as he feared, the answers were the same from around the table. No. It didn't take him long to get to the front door of the house. He looked outside and her Jeep was parked in exactly the same spot it had been since the day they ladies arrived.

Concern rippled through him. Where was she? He went back into the kitchen where everyone was finishing up their breakfast. "Did anyone here her leave the house in the night or this morning?"

Again, the same answer. No.

Tay looked up and smiled. "Maybe she just went for a walk. She knew we'd be leaving today."

"Maybe so, but I'm going to find out for sure." His heart was in his throat, but why? There was no indication anything had happened to her, but he wanted to be damned positive.

Outside, he glanced around the property and checked all of the out buildings before he headed to the barn. He went straight to Samantha's empty stall and all of his worst fears came to life. Stacy had gone for a ride. Alone. Damnit!

She was a good rider, but she didn't know the area well enough to go out by herself. He had to find her.

He ran toward the house. "Hal, Joe Ray!"

Joe Ray scurried out the back door with Hal and Brian right behind. "What's up, D."

"She's gone. Stacy's gone. She took Sammy out for a ride. We need to find her before she gets lost or something worse." He didn't want to think that something could have happened to her out there all alone, but he couldn't help it. He knew what it was like to get hurt riding and he only prayed nothing like that had taken place.

Daron saddled his horse as fast as he could. "Hal, you go east, I'll go west, Brian, north and Joe Ray, south."

It felt like a scene from an old western movie as he handed each of the hands a holster and a pistol. "Put these on. If you find her and she's okay, shoot into the air one time. If she's hurt, shoot twice. That will help the rest of us find you."

"Are you that worried, D?" Hal asked.

"I'd rather be safe than sorry, that's all. If no one spots her within an hour, let's meet back here and we'll go to plan B."

"What's that, Daron?" Brian put the holster on his belt and mounted his horse.

"We'll have to get the chopper out and search by air. Now let's get it boys." He knew he could count on his hands to do exactly what he asked. He only hoped they would find her safe and sound and wouldn't have to do a more serious search.

He'd gotten his pilots licenses when he was in L.A. Not only had he been a stunt horseback rider for Universal Studio, but he'd been a stunt pilot as well. It had come in handy a few times rounding up cattle. He never dreamed he'd be thinking of using the machine for a rescue. No...that wasn't going to happen, she was going to be safe. He felt it in his heart, or was it just hope?

* * *

Stacy had thought Samantha saw a snake, but it was a false alarm and now she relished in the warmth of the sun as she rode back toward the ranch. She was sure everyone had eaten by now and the girls would be packed and ready to go. It had been a longer ride than she'd expected to take, and she loved every minute of it.

The barn was in view, but she didn't see anyone milling around outside. Maybe Sunday morning was one of rest around the ranch and everyone was inside. Either way, she would unsaddle Sammy and let her cool off before she groomed her and went inside to get ready to leave.

Funny, the barn door was open and Daron's horse, along with the rest of the guys mounts, was gone. Maybe they had decided to take an early morning ride, too.

Maybe they'd stay gone long enough that she wouldn't have to say an empty goodbye to Daron. It might make it easier if she didn't have to look into his blue eyes again.

"Sammy, let's get you settled then I'm going to make a run for the house and get the heck out of dodge before the guys get back."

The sudden sound of pounding horse's hooves against the hard ground startled her. What was going on? Daron was shouting orders, but she could only hear bits and pieces.

"Hanger…helicopter…four wheeler…Sherriff…"

Something was terribly wrong. She dropped the grooming brush to the floor, ran out the stall, down the breezeway to the outdoors. Everyone was scrambling, until they saw her. Then as if in slow motion, they all stopped and stared at her.

She met each one of their concerned gaze, then held her hands out in question. "What? What's wrong?"

Daron dashed toward her and grabbed her. She thought his embrace would crush the life out of her.

"Are you alright?" He held her at arm's length and studied her up and down.

The frantic sound of his voice almost didn't register. Then she realized what he'd said. She moved out of his embrace. "Of course I'm all right. What's wrong with you?"

His concerned look took on a darker appearance. She didn't like what she saw as the others gathered around.

"Where were you?"

"I went for a ride, so what? I don't know what the big deal is."

"I'll tell you what the big deal is, Miss Priss. You left without telling anyone where you were going. It wasn't a very responsible thing to do. What if you'd gotten hurt? None of us knew which direction you went in and you don't know this country well enough not to get lost. You scared the hell out of all of us, that's what the big deal is."

She didn't appreciate his tone one bit. Who did he think he was? "First of all, Mr. Tyler, my name is Miss Jones and I'm not your child so you won't tell me what to do. Secondly, I believe I found my way back here quite well. Third, I don't think I have to 'check in' with you, or anyone else for that matter, for anything I do. So I guess everyone worried for nothing. And last but not least, you will never have to worry about me doing anything around here again, because I'm leaving."

She turned away from him and started toward the house. Aware of the opened mouths of the hands, Lupe and Manuel, she fought the urge to run. She couldn't run, she had to keep her dignity. How on earth had such a great week come to this?

Take a simple, early morning ride. That's all she'd done. Nothing less, nothing more, and damn him for treating her like an adolescent. He was an overbearing oaf and she'd be relieved to be away from him. How could she have ever thought she was in love with such a bully? She was happy his true colors had shown before she left. Now she knew she could get over him, and quickly.

The back door of the house slammed harder than she'd intended when she entered. With no one around, she ran to her room, shut the door behind her and fell onto the sofa.

Hot tears burned her eyes. She tried to keep them at bay to no avail. Why? Why had he treated her like that?

The sound of his panicked voice came back to her and the relieved look on his face when he'd first seen her shot through her mind.

He had really been afraid something had happened to her, and so were all the others. Why else would they have been out looking for her?

She sat up, wiped her face with the back of her hands and tried to calm her sobs. Sugarbear licked the salty liquid from her skin, and did her best to comfort her master. "Oh, Sugar, what a fool I am. Daron is absolutely right. It was stupid of me to leave and not tell anyone where I was going. And if

I'd have gotten hurt, it would have been my own fault."

Her tears subsided as the little dog jumped into her lap. "Poor Lupe and the others, they must have been worried sick."

She dried the remainder of her tears and stood. "I'm going to pack and load my things, then I'll apologize to everyone."

Thankful Tay and Whitley didn't go into the mornings happenings in depth, Stacy shut the back door of her SUV. It was time to say her goodbyes and apologize for her childish behavior. She only hoped she could do it without crying.

She turned out of the great room and into the kitchen. Relieved to see Lupe and Manuel were the only ones in the room, she walked over to the older woman and put her arms around her. "Lupe, I'm so sorry about going off like that. It never crossed my mind that it was the wrong thing to do."

"It's okay. Sometimes we don't think before we act. That goes for all of us." Lupe forced her to meet her gaze. "All of us. Even grown men sometimes do things out of desperation."

Stacy knew what Lupe was trying to say, but it was too late. Even though Daron had been right about what he'd said, he had no right to talk to her like that. But that was neither here nor there. It was over now.

She smiled at the older couple she'd come to love. "Thank you two for everything. I'll remember you always." She turned, gave Manuel a hug and said, "Goodbye now." then left the room to go find

Hal, Joe Ray and Brian with Sugarbear hot on her heels.

"Hey, guys," she said when she saw the three gathered in the open area at the back of the barn. It was the same place they stood the first time she'd seen them.

"I just want to apologize for the ruckus this morning. I was wrong for what I did and I know you rode hard to try to find me."

"No harder than the D-man did, ma'am." Joe Ray gave her a hug.

She was pleased to feel forgiveness from every one of the hands as one by one they hugged her and said their goodbyes. The men walked out of the barn together and she made her way to Samantha's stall. She wanted to brush her one last time before she left.

Sammy greeted her with a nuzzle to her neck. When Stacy stepped into the stall, someone grabbed her and pulled her toward them. Within a heartbeat, Daron's lips were on hers. His embrace was tender yet commanding. Another oxymoron.

With fain objection, she tried to wiggle free of his hold. The passion of his kiss stopped her protest and she allowed herself to calm in his arms. She heard Sugarbear's happy bark somewhere in the background of her mind. It was all like a dream.

When his lips left hers he held her close and whispered in her ear, "I don't know what I'd have done if something would have happened to you out there. It made me realize just how much you mean to me. I know now that you are the only woman I could, or will, ever love."

He let his embrace loosen just enough for their gazes to meet. His blue eyes blazed with wanting and desire. "Can you forgive me for overreacting? I was just so scared I might lose you, I was out of my mind with worry."

At this moment, she could forgive the man anything. He'd said he loved her. Halleluiah, he loved her!

She glanced down and fumbled with a button on his shirt. "Well..." The air was charged with silence.

"Did you hear me, Stacy, I said, I love you."

With all of her heart and soul, she knew he meant what he said. She gazed into the most beautiful eyes of any man. "And I love you."

Their lips met once again and she knew her early morning adventure had been the ride of a lifetime.

NO ROOM TO SPARE

D'Lacy stepped out of her car and marveled at the beauty of the quaint bed and breakfast. "The Inn at Harbor Ridge," she whispered. What a beautiful place and so quiet.

It was the first time she'd been to the Lake of the Ozarks and she loved it already. The aroma of pine, fresh cut grass and honeysuckle met her senses. It was so much different than the odor of car exhaust that hovered over the City.

The quiet of the Ozark Mountains was calming. Who was she fooling? Anything was calming compared to the noises that invaded her ears as a City inhabitant. Even though her home town of Kansas City, Missouri was considered to be in the Ozarks, it was nothing like this.

The sun began to retreat behind the horizon. A light supper, hot bath, glass of red wine and a good night's sleep were the only things on her agenda for the evening. The writers' conference she was to attend the next day would a long one and she wanted her senses sharp.

Jaymon Vance, the Keynote speaker, was a bestselling author and she didn't want to miss one minute of his speech. She had always wanted to be a writer and had toyed with it during high school and college, but once she started teaching, it seemed the dream had flown out the window.

That wasn't true and she knew it. It wasn't teaching that halted her writing. After the bitter breakup with her boyfriend of three years, she realized who had put a stop to it, but now wasn't the time to think of her ex's cheating ass. However, his actions made her realize she didn't love him anymore. Somehow, she wondered if she ever had.

Oh, well, it didn't matter. School was out, she was off for the summer and she was going to follow her dream. Something he had never allowed her to do.

"Stop it, Lace," she scolded herself. "Put that man, all men for that matter, out of your mind and enjoy your weekend." The corners of her mouth lifted at herself chiding. Talking to herself was a habit she'd gotten into as a child. Apparently, it was a hard one to break.

She chuckled and walked along the concrete path to the bed and breakfast. The beige colored two-story home had green shutters and a large porch that went across the front. It was surrounded by flowers of all shapes, sizes and colors. A big red barn sat to the back of the house and was bordered by a white rail fence. It looked as if it, as well as the main house, had rooms.

One of the large trees in perfectly groomed yard of the house had a wrought iron bench underneath inviting her to sit and enjoy her surroundings, but that bath was calling to her.

Entering the front door, she found her way to the desk. A young lady stood in front of a computer with a phone to her ear.

"I'll be with you shortly." The girl said typing something on the keyboard then she placed the receiver in its cradle. "I'm sorry for the wait. I just came on shift and the phone hasn't stopped ringing."

"That's okay. My name's D'Lacy Mason. I have reservations for the weekend."

"Hi, I'm Sue. I'm glad you made reservations. We're so booked because of the writer's conference folks have been calling and coming in, and we have absolutely no rooms left." Sue typed on the computer keyboard once again. "That goes for every B&B, hotel and motel on the Lake. Everyone is booked. Yes, there you are." She reached into a box on the back wall. You're room is in the Big Red Barn."

"Oh?" She was hoping to stay in the main house, but she didn't want to gripe. At least she had a room.

"Yes, you'll love it. You're in 'A Roll in the Hay' room. It has a nice private deck, a hot tub and a lot more amenities. Too bad you'll be there alone. It's a romantic room."

"Romance is something I'm definitely not looking for, but thanks for the thought." She took the key Sue offered. "What? No electronic keys?"

"Nope, we do it the old fashion way, real door keys."

"That's refreshing. Hey, am I allowed to get a bottle of Cabernet from the lounge and take it to my room?"

"Sure, matter of fact, you don't have to go and get it. I'll give you time to get settled and send room service with it."

Sue handed her had directions to parking and to her room. She couldn't wait to get in that hot tub.

* * *

D'Lacy pulled her bag behind her as she searched for her room. A man stood at a door ahead of her attempting to turn a key in the knob. Wait! What was he doing? That was her room he was trying to get into.

"Excuse me, sir, I believe you may be trying to wrong door. This is my room."

Five foot nine herself, when he stood to his full height she saw that he was at least six foot. His green eyes sparkled and his smile showed straight white teeth.

Shaking his head from side to side he replied. "No, ma'am, this is my room, I just can't seem to get the door open."

He ran his fingers through dark blonde hair and she felt her breath catch when she tried to inhale. Damn, he was handsome. Stop it right now. There it was again, her self discipline. At least this time she hadn't said it out loud. So what if he was good looking? He was still trying to get into her room.

She looked at the room name on her key chain, then at the name above the door. "A Roll in the Hay, this is my room." She stepped in front of him, put her key in, turned the knob and opened the door.

"See?" She stepped into the room, but he gently grasped her arm and stopped her. She glanced down at his hand then shot him a warning look. How dare he put his hands on her? He must have read into her gaze exactly what she'd intended.

He let go of her and stuffed his hand in his pocket. "Sorry. Your key fitting is all well and good, but unfortunately, my key chain says the same thing yours does"

Reading the words printed on the green diamond shaped plastic, she realized he had told her the truth. She also noticed her arm tingled where he'd touched her and warmth spread into her shoulder. Oh, no. She closed her eyes and swallowed hard. The signs of this meeting pointed to one thing only. Get this figured out and get away from him as soon as possible.

She'd been attracted to men before, but never had anyone's first touch affected her in this way. Get yourself together Lace and stop thinking like that. Okay, enough was enough.

"There must be some kind of mix up." What was she going to do now? This was absurd! Surely they had given him that key by mistake. Well, she had no other choice. "Come in and I'll call the desk to see which room is really yours."

He followed close behind. "Maybe you should ask them which room is really yours. I believe I arrived first, so if there is a mix up, the room is actually mine."

"We'll see about that." She picked up the phone, dialed zero and waited for someone to answer. "Yes, this is Miss Mason in A Roll in the Hay."

The low chuckle that came from behind her made her even more aware of what the room name meant, and heat rushed to her face. "No, I said A Roll in the Hay." Now she was twice as embarrassed.

"Is this Sue? Well, we have a little problem." She glanced in the tall man's direction. "No, Sue, we have a big problem. There's a gentleman here who claims this is his room. However, his key doesn't fit into the door, so I was wondering if you could find out which room is really his so I can get on with my evening.

"Okay, hold on." She looked up at the man beside her. Amusement was written on his handsome face and all she wanted to do was slap it off. What did he think was so funny? "You're name?"

"Huh?"

"I need your name." She heard her own sarcasm.

His voice was pleasant and laced with humor, "Vance, Jaymon Vance."

Who? Her heart stopped for a split second then threatened to jump free of its boundaries. Jaymon Vance? The Keynote speaker for the conference? "Excuse me?" Why she said that she didn't know. She'd heard him loud and clear.

He put his hands in the air and formed the

words in sign language as he spoke, "III saaiid myyy naaaame issss Jayyyyymonnn Vannnnccccce."

Why him? The lump that had formed in her throat went down hard. Are you going to let him talk to you like that? It didn't matter who he was, Jaymon Vance or Joe Blow, she didn't like his attitude. "Smart ass."

She turned her attention back to the phone. "His name is Jaymon Vance, Sue. Hurry and look him up so he can get on with his evening, too."

"What?" She couldn't believe what she was hearing. "That's impossible." She felt more than saw Jaymon Vance move closer to her. His warmth penetrated her clothing and heated her skin. It was her imagination; he was too far away for that to be happening.

"No, I made my reservations for both Friday and Saturday night. Just a minute, let me look." The receiver clanked against the bed side table when she put it down.

Jaymon took a seat in a very comfortable looking chair. "What's the problem?"

Though his words were those of sarcasm, she knew he didn't mean them that way and was only teasing her. However, this was serious. If she made the mistake Sue had said, she was stuck without a room for the night.

Purse in hand, she sat on the bed and rummaged through it. The piece of paper in her hand told it all. Her heart sank to the pit of her stomach as she once again picked up the telephone receiver.

"You're right, Sue, I did only make

reservations for Saturday night. Yes, I know there are no rooms anywhere on the lake. No, it's not your fault. It was my mistake. The only thing I can do is drive back to Eldon or Clarksburg and trust there's a room there. I agree, I don't want to go all the way back to KC. Okay, thanks."

What was she supposed to do now? If there weren't any rooms in nearby towns then what? She'd cross that bridge when she came to it.

The handle of her bag was cool when she grabbed it.

Jaymon watched the lovely lady hang up the phone. Her hair glistened as the sun stole one last ray through the window before taking its leave for the night. Bright auburn locks hung over her shoulders and he fought the urge to touch the softness of their waves. "Not your room after all, huh?"

"No, Mr. Vance, it's yours." She began to walk away. He couldn't just let her leave. It wouldn't be right. Hell, he didn't even know her given name.

She reminded him of someone he'd like to characterize in one of his books. Beautiful, spunky, intelligent, and had he already thought of beautiful? He wasn't sure, but stunning might be a better word.

He stepped in her way when she started for the door. "I'm afraid we got off to a bad start, miss…"

"Mason. Yes we did, but apparently, I am the one who was in the wrong. My apologies, sir."

She attempted to maneuver around him, but again he stepped in her way. Why? Why was he hesitant to let her go?

"Listen, Miss Mason. I have an idea. Are you here for the writers' conference tomorrow?" She was standing so close the faint aroma of Jasmine radiated to his nostrils. He was tempted to breathe deeper so he could inhale more of her.

"Yes."

"Then, look." He pointed to the sofa. "That makes out into a bed. Why don't we just share the room for the night? I'll sleep on the sofa bed and you can have the regular bed. Problem solved."

It was a long shot, but the least he could do was try to help her out. Was that the real reason he wanted her to stay, to help her? Or was it for his own selfish reasons?

His deepest concern was the affect she had on him. The way he felt when he peered into her blue eyes, even more, the way his body reacted when he'd barely touched her. Damn, now he wished he hadn't asked. What was he thinking?

"Tell me truthfully, Mr. Vance, do you really expect me to stay in a room with a man I don't even know?"

"You tell me truthfully, Miss Mason, what are your other options? What if you get to Clarksburg and there are no rooms there either? Where are you going to sleep? In your car? Do you really want to make the three hour drive back to Kansas City, then turn right around and come back in the morning?" Why was he still trying to convince her to stay, and why did he care where she slept?

"What do I know about you except you're Jaymon Vance, the well-known, New York Times bestselling author. I assume you're not some demented serial killer, though the mysteries you write scare the hell out of me."

"Good, that's what they're intended to do." He hesitated. "I can the wheels turning in your head," he said with a smile. "Here," He reached for a three partition divider that sat in front of the hot tub. "I'll put this between the bed and the hide-a-way. At least it will be a little more private." He knew she was pondering his proposition.

"Mr. Vance—"

"Please, call me Jaymon."

"I really appreciate the offer, but this is not your problem and you shouldn't have to give up your own privacy because of my stupidity."

He didn't have time for this. Deadlines, public appearances, meetings with editors, publishers, agents, his agenda in general wouldn't permit him occasion for a relationship. Relationship? Now he was thinking in terms he couldn't allow.

He'd put up all the fight he was going to. If she wanted to leave, she was right, it wasn't his problem. He stepped toward the door and reached for the knob. "I hope you have a blanket with you. It might get cool sleeping in your car." That came off colder than he'd intended, but what the hell.

The bastard! But, he was right, if she had to sleep in her car, as well as being chilly, she'd probably be scared. At least there were people around here that would hear her scream if she had to.

"You know what, Mr. Van…" She cleared her

throat. "I mean, Jaymon. You are arrogant, rude and probably self-centered. But! You have a good point and I'll take you up on your offer."

"Thanks for the compliments."

"Smart ass."

"Again you call me a smart ass, when like you said, you don't even know me." He offered her a handshake. "Maybe we should start all over. Hi, my name's Jaymon Vance, and you are?"

Now she wanted to giggle like a school girl. What in the world had gotten into her? Whatever it was, she had to make the best of the situation, so she may as well be cordial. "D'Lacy Mason, but my friends call me Lacy."

She took his hand and was immediately sorry. Electric currents shot up her arm and headed straight for her heart. What was this night going to bring?

"Well, my friends call me Jay." He turned toward his bag and unzipped it. "We may as well start our Roll in the Hay."

Butterflies danced in her stomach. What have you gotten yourself into?

CHAPTER 2

"*G*rowl why don't you?" Lacy said to her stomach as she opened her suitcase. It was seven in the evening and she was famished. "Well, so much for your light supper, hot bath and glass of wine, Lace."

She looked into her bag and right on top of her cotton nightgown laid a book. A mystery she'd picked up at the book store just before she left for Lake of the Ozarks. She read the title. 'The Unwelcome Guest'… by Jay Vance. How ironic.

Picking up the hardback she glanced out the window of the sliding glass door at its author. It was really him, Jay Vance, sitting on the deck simply moving back and forth in a rocking chair looking regal. No, that wasn't regal, it was arrogant. She couldn't forget that. No matter how good looking he was or how nice he seemed, he was still an arrogant bastard! "Keep that in mind Lace. If for no other reason, to protect your heart," she whispered.

The man outside stood and walked toward the door. She turned quickly. Did he catch her looking at him? Her heart raced. She had to hide the book before he saw it. Air refused to go into her lungs, it was too late.

"Oh, I see you have my latest creation."

He stepped up beside her and when he put his hand out, she willingly handed the book to him. His fingertips brushed against hers for a scant moment, but the heat it caused in her body lasted much longer. Damn the spice of his aftershave. It was just enough to tickle her senses and a tingle ran down her spine. She tried to step away, but he moved in unison with her.

"What do you think about this cover?" he asked, "I'm not crazy about it, but I only get to give my ideas. They do the rest."

He held the book under the yellow glow of the lamp. A figure lurked in the shadows of a cozy living room. Blood dripped from the blade of a butcher knife and stained the floor below.

The scene gave her the creeps but it was a mystery. "It looks okay to me. Is that the unwanted guest standing there?"

He handed the book back to her and lifted her chin with his finger. She met his emerald gaze. Was he going to kiss her?

"If I told you, I'd have to kill you." He dropped his hand and walked away.

She held her tongue, but it was all she could do not to call him a smart ass again. Warmth lingered on her chin where he'd touched her. How could he infuriate her and make her want him at the same time? And why did she think he was going to kiss her? In her subconscious did she want him to kiss her? But even a bigger question was why, when she'd only known him so such a short time, did he bring out emotions in her no one else had?

A knock at the door brought her a start. "Who could that be?"

"I don't know, but I'll get it."

She marveled at the way his muscles worked beneath his clothing as he leisurely walked toward the door. When he opened the door, the words from the other side propelled her feet to move forward.

"Your wine sir."

Turning toward her, Jay smiled and said. "Wine? Did you order wine for us, darling?"

Darling! Was he trying to make the room service waiter think they were together in this room, alone? Dummy, you are in this room together… alone.

She made a quick stop at her purse before she continued to doorway. How had she forgotten to tell Sue to cancel the wine! She hurried to the door, took the bottle and cork screw from the young man and gave him a tip. "Don't mind my brother, he's mentally ill."

"Oh, ah, yes ma'am, and thank you."

A perceptive smile on the server's face told her he had heard such stories before and didn't believe a word of what she'd said.

The door closed harder than she'd intended. She scooted around Jay and set the bottle on the small kitchen table that had settings for two already in place.

Aware he had come to stand beside her she closed her eyes and swallowed hard. The embarrassment she felt at that moment was incredible, as was her want for the stranger nearby. His voice was low and friendly.

"Are you hungry?" He picked up the wine bottle and studied the label. "Hmm, good choice."

She met his gaze the best she could. 'Listen, my foolishness brought this on. I was so excited to attend my first writers' conference with my favorite author as the Keynote speaker I made reservations too far in advance. I simply forgot I was going to drive in tomorrow morning and only spend one night."

"So what's your point?"

There was that arrogance again or was it playfulness? Whatever it was, it irritated her. "You don't have to be nice. Just ignore me as if I weren't here, Mr. Vance."

Ignore her? That was one thing he definitely couldn't do. Her every move heightened his awareness of her closeness and he didn't want the opportunity to get to know her better, to slip through his fingers.

He sat the wine down. "So, we're back to Mr. Vance are we?" He walked toward the bed side table and picked up the room service menu.

"Miss Mason, right?" As if he didn't know her name. He watched her nod her beautiful head. "So you goofed up. We all goof up now and again, some more than others, but we have to learn from our mistakes and move on."

There it was again, that spark that flickered in her blue eyes when she became annoyed with him. He wanted to smile, but couldn't allow it. Just because she was so beautiful when she frowned at him like that gave him no right to amuse himself.

Giving her a hard time was fun but if he wanted to learn more about her it would have to stop. "Okay, I'm sorry. I'm just kidding, Lacy. Really, I'm starving. We're here so, we may as well take advantage of having company for supper."

Whatever it took, from that moment forward it would be his priority to make her feel comfortable. What the hell, it was only for the weekend. "Well? You haven't answered my question. Are you hungry?" He was pleased when she visibly relaxed.

"Well… Yes, but I'll order only on one condition."

"What's that?"

"You let me buy."

"Okay by me."

"Then show me that menu. My stomach's been growling so much I'm afraid it's going to start barking."

Lacy wanted to hide under the table after that statement, but the sound of Jay's laughter was infectious and she joined in. Thankful that some of the ice between them had been chipped away, she was more at ease. Besides, it would be nice if she could pick his brain on his writing expertise. What better chance would she have then over supper?

The aroma of mesquite grilled steak filled the suite. Jay had opened the wine and poured them a glass while they waited for their meal to arrive. Now, they sat at the table while the waiter served them from the small roller cart that held the food.

It was cozy and, though she hated to admit it, romantic. The wine made her more receptive to the circumstances and she found herself enjoying it. It was like a date, which admittedly she hadn't had one of in a while.

The server placed the last of the morsels on the table and poured them each another glass of wine. "Is there anything else I can get you folks?"

"I believe that's it." Jay answered then followed the young man to the door. "We'll call if we need to."

The tall man, who was her roommate for the night, closed the door, made his way back to the table then took his place across from her. He'd taken off his shoes and unbuttoned his shirt revealing his white undershirt. If she'd thought he was handsome before, now, in this relaxed setting, he was actually sexy. Maybe the wine made her think that way, but whatever it was, she liked it.

She cut her steak which showed the perfect amount of pink in the middle. "Mmmmm, this is delicious." She closed her eyes and savored the taste.

A comfortable silence exuded through the room as they ate. Small talk was scarce, but good company wasn't. She found herself steeling glances at Jay and noticed him doing the same.

He laid his fork on his plate and took his last

sip of wine then looked at his watch. "I didn't realize how late it's gotten. It's almost 9:00. I have some homework to do before tomorrow." He met her gaze. "Are you finished eating?"

Red wine was her favorite and it went down smooth. She placed her glass on the table. "Yes and it was wonderful." Did he know she meant being with him was wonderful?

"That it was, girl." He stood and began stacking the dishes.

She pushed her chair back and pitched in. It was funny how it all came so natural. The wine, Lace, the wine, it's a false security blanket. Whatever, she was going to enjoy it. "This is my first conference and I can't wait to hear your speech in the morning."

"How long have you been writing?"

"I'm almost embarrassed to answer."

"Why's that?" He piled the dished in the small sink of the kitchenette.

"I have a story in mind, but so far, I haven't written a word. I just don't know how to start, or where to start for that matter. I wrote some pieces years ago, but nothing since college."

"The first thing I do after I come up with a plot idea is get to know my characters. Where they're from, what they do, who their parents are or were, that kind of thing."

"That sounds reasonable." She tilted her head upward and met his gaze. The softness behind she saw showed her a little more about the man standing beside her. She couldn't bring herself to look away, mesmerized by his voice, his eyes his very presents.

He took a step closer. "The better you become acquainted with your characters, the easier it is to grow with them and love them as the story unfolds."

"I see," were the only words she could muster. He was close, so close she was tempted to take it upon herself to kiss him, but that would be too brazen. Or would it? She was so confused.

Damn, she was beautiful. Her perfectly shaped lips all but demanded attention from his. Her blue eyes smoldered. Was that want he saw in her eyes?

The wine, the romantic setting and the entire circumstance was taking him aback. No, he knew it wasn't any of that. It was the woman standing there that affected him. The beautiful creature he longed to hold in his arms.

He had to shake these feelings. He was to busy for these thoughts to invade his heart and mind. He had work to do before morning and a contract to fulfill.

"Well! It looks like I'd better get started on my last minute preparations for tomorrow." Turning away from Lacy Mason was one of the hardest things he'd forced himself to do in a long, long time. Even her name held an aura of loveliness around it that he adored.

"Y-yes, I guess you'd better. I'll finish up here."

Was that a flicker of disappointment he read in her eyes? He wouldn't let himself read something into her actions that wasn't there. Just because he was infatuated with her, didn't mean she was with him.

He picked up his laptop case and after she wiped off the table he went through the motions of getting ready to do his work. However in his peripheral vision, his focus was on her. She took some toiletries out of her bag and a soft cotton nightgown lay over her arm. His book rested on the bed side table.

She repositioned the room divider to block his view of where she'd be sleeping. It didn't matter if he could see her or not, his imagination would take control. Being blessed with a vivid imagination was great when it came to his writing, but in this case, it might drive him insane.

The laptop screen came to life and he opened the necessary file. His speech for the next day only needed a little tweaking before it would be ready.

Lacy stepped toward the bathroom door. "I'm going to take a quick bath then go to bed. I'll try not to disturb you."

It was too late for that. Already his thoughts were filled with her and he fought to concentrate on his work. "Okay, this won't take long, then I'm going to hit the sack myself."

"Is that what you're going to talk to us about tomorrow?"

"Uh-hum."

"Want to give me a sneak preview?

"It's about the basics of writing like manuscript setup, finding an agent, plotting your story, stuff like that."

"Just what I need. I'll leave you to it."

He heard the door shut behind her and the click

of the lock. Placing his hands behind his head, he sat back in his chair and inhaled a deep breath through his nose and exhaled out his mouth. Why was he so attracted to the woman in the next room?

It wasn't because he was deprived of female companionship. Being a single man in his business wasn't easy. Women threw themselves at him all the time. He realized it wasn't him they were after. Not the real person that he was, but they wanted the man behind the book covers, the celebrity and glamour they believed his life held.

Until now, he'd blamed not having a meaningful relationship on lack of time. However, he wondered if it was because he hadn't seen in other women what he saw in Lacy. What made her different?

He didn't know, but what he did recognize was he needed to direct his thoughts elsewhere. A woman in his life wasn't something he needed right now. He wouldn't be able to devote himself to her like he knew he should. It would be hard, but he would have to distance himself from this intriguing woman.

The sound of water rushing into the tub slowed to a stopped and sweet Jasmine wafted from underneath the bathroom door. He closed his eyes and enjoyed the flowered aroma knowing he couldn't get close to the skin that wore it. It was going to be a long night.

.

CHAPTER 3

*A*fter applying her lipstick, Lacy tossed the tube in her purse then worked at getting mascara to cover her light strawberry blond eyelashes.

"Damnit!" She grabbed a tissue and wiped at the black smudge beneath her eye. "If you had dark lashes, you wouldn't have to use so much of this stuff. Now look at what you've done." The tissue smeared a streak down her cheek.

She studied her reflection in the mirror. "You're a real piece of work, you know that? I think Jay Vance has gotten under your skin. That's why you're nerves are on end. Thankfully, you don't have to sleep so close to him tonight."

A chuckle escaped her lips. "You dummy, if you don't stop talking to yourself, one day, someone's going to catch you and put you in a loony bin."

"Hey, sorry to interrupt your chat, but I forgot my shower radio."

Her heart thumped against her chest and she jumped at the low tone of Jay's voice. Turning toward the bathroom door, she peered into his green eyes and consciously had to close her gaping mouth. When had he come in, and exactly how much of her 'chat' had he heard? "Ah, wah... ah..." His smile did nothing to ease her anxiety.

"So you talk to yourself?" He said as he reached inside the shower and retrieved the waterproof radio.

She blinked and swallowed the bile that rose in her throat. She wanted to answer his question by saying no, but the word wouldn't come out. Why couldn't she do anything but stand there looking at him?

He picked up a hand towel and wiped the excess water from the electronic device. "Sometimes it's comforting, isn't it? Talking to yourself I mean."

What? He talked to himself too? No way. Surely he was just saying that to make her feel better. Why the hell didn't he leave? The closeness of the small bathroom, his unique musky sent and his green eyes did little to still her racing pulse.

The towel again in its rightful place, Jay turned and met her gaze. "See you in a few."

All she could do was nod as she watched him walk away. She let out the breath she didn't realize she'd been holding, relaxed back and rested her bottom on the edge of the vanity. "Okay, what just happened?" Was she losing her mind? She just talked to herself again.

She left her makeup on the vanity and went into

the kitchen, poured herself a cup of the coffee that Jay had so graciously made earlier, and sat at the table. Glancing into the other room, she looked at the hide-a-bed where Jay slept the night before and wondered what it would have been like laying there next to him.

"Wait a minute." She realized his suitcase and all of his belongings, even the radio he claimed he'd left, were still lying on the bed. "What the...?" Wasn't she supposed to have the room for tonight? "What's going on here?"

She glanced at her watch and realized she didn't have time to contact the front desk and wondered how long she'd been daydreaming. She grabbed her keys from her purse and made a mad dash out the door. "After all I've been through to be at this conference, the last thing I'm going to do is miss Jay Vance's Keynote speech."

* * *

Jay scanned the large room for Lacy. It was almost time for him to begin his presentation and he knew she wanted to hear it. He hoped him walking in on her while she was talking to herself hadn't embarrassed her to the point of not attending the conference.

She looked vulnerable and shocked when he appeared at the bathroom door. She was so beautiful standing there not knowing what to do or say. All he wanted to do was pull her in his arms and kiss her sweet lips.

He wished he had told her he was used to

women in his life talking to their selves? Hell, not only did his mother do it, but his little sister had the same trait. It was something he'd grown up with, but he also knew that neither one of them liked for anyone outside the family to hear them. They were afraid they would be deemed crazy or something.

The conference coordinator approached the podium. "Good morning writers…"

Where the hell was Lacy? Now he was getting worried. He scanned the room once again. Maybe he'd just missed seeing her the first time. No, he would have recognized those blue eyes and long red waves atop her head anywhere.

"…We have some wonderful speakers for you today…"

Fear bubbled in Jay's stomach. What if it wasn't that she didn't come because he'd caught her talking to herself? What if something had happened to her, what if she'd been hurt somehow? No, he couldn't let himself think that.

"…Let's have a big round of applause for Mr. Jay Vance."

He swallowed hard and pulled his thoughts back to his task at hand. However, as soon as his speech was over, he was going to find out where Miss D'Lacy Mason was and make sure she was alright.

His hour long speech seemed a lot longer, but he glanced at his watch for the umpteenth time and indeed it had only been sixty minutes. Time wasted that he could have been looking for Lacy. He gave out the last of his handouts.

The gnawing at his heart from not knowing if

she was safe was driving him crazy. Why was he so concerned about someone he'd just met? He had never believed in love at first sight, but now he wasn't sure. Could he be in love?

He'd watched the door more than he'd made eye contact with the conference goers and wondered if he had hidden well enough the fact that something was bothering him.

"This is a list of the Agents I told you about earlier. Don't be afraid to submit your manuscript. Your agent is your doorway to getting published.

Finally, it was over. "My thanks to the Ozarks Writers League for asking me to speak today and I'd like to come back again. Thank you very much."

He hardly heard the applause as he gathered his papers and stepped away from the podium. One last glance at the door and his heart sank to his stomach. Lacy walked in and he could tell she'd been crying.

* * *

Lacy wiped what she hoped was the last of her tears away as she walked into the conference room. All eyes had been on Jay, so hopefully no one noticed her.

"How could this happen. Today of all days" Her heart was broken, however, when she saw Jay coming toward her with concern on his face, her heart spirits a little.

His touch made an electrical current run up her arm as he took her hand. Where were they going? She didn't care as long as Jay was with her. He led her into a small secluded area off the side of the conference room and she followed willingly.

He placed his things on a small table then turned to face her. "Where have you been?"

His voice wasn't scolding, but worried. That was all it took, her tears came readily again. "I-I had a little accident." She watched as he scanned her body.

"Are you okay?"

"Yes, it wasn't bad."

"What happened, was it your fault?"

"No. Some elderly lady ran into the back of my car while I was stopped at a red light. That caused me to bump into the guy in front of me."

"But no one was hurt?"

She sniffed as he took her face in his hands and wiped away her tears with his thumbs. He was so close his warm breath brushed on her lips. "No." When she met his gaze there was something akin to passion there. In the blink of an eye, their lips met. Everything around them disappeared and she was in her own little world, a world that would never be the same. Cupid's arrow flew and landed directly in the middle of her heart. At that moment she knew she was in love with Jay Vance.

Never had she been kissed like that. When he dropped his hands from her face and took her in his arms, she welcomed his embrace. It felt right, natural, safe. She didn't want the moment to end, but their lips parted and his voice was low and husky.

"I was so worried about you."

"Really?"

"I thought you weren't coming because I

caught you talking to yourself."

Oh, god, he actually brought it up. "I don't do that all the time." She was so ashamed. Why did she routinely do that? It was hard for her to look at him.

He placed a finger under her chin and forced her to meed his gaze. "Listen, don't be embarrassed. My mom and my sister talk to themselves. I'm used to it."

The shrug of his shoulders and the look on his face let her know the words came from his heart. He was telling the truth. What a relief to know she wasn't the only one in the world that had that weird habit, but was that why he'd kissed her like the way he did?

"That makes me feel better. I've always had a complex about that."

"Well, don't."

The kiss, it kept haunting her. "Ah, is that the only reason? I mean, because of… you know… me talking to myself?"

"No, there's another reason."

His grin caused her heart to skip a beat. "What? What's the other rea--"

"Because, I think I love you."

Surely her heart was going to explode. Had he really said the words? Words she'd longed to hear from the man that held her in his arms? Their gazes were locked. He peered into her soul and she welcomed it. Her voice was just above a whisper. "Say it again."

His green eyes twinkled and the corner of his mouth lifted in a half grin. He was the most handsome man she'd ever seen.

"I love you,"

Yes! She had heard him right. She's said and heard those three words before, but they now really held a meaning. "Can I tell you something?" She watched his mischievous grin fade.

"Do I want to hear it?"

"I think so."

"Then, tell me."

"I love you, too."

The smile on his face brought a smile to hers. His lips took hers once again and she longed-for the emotions she felt to never end. This feeling was something she hadn't experienced before, but then, she'd never been in love. When their lips parted for the second time and his breath was warm to her ear as he whispered.

"If you wrecked your car how did you get here?"

"My car doesn't have much damage, so I drove."

He held her closer. "Then, why are you crying?"

Tears welled in her eyes again. "Because I missed your presentation, and it was the one thing I really wanted to hear."

"Then, you meant what you said last night?"

"What?"

"That I am your favorite author."

"Yeah, well, don't let it go to your head."

"You know, if you could drive correctly, you would have been here for my speech."

She gave him a light punch to the ribs. "Smart ass."

A low rumble came from deep within Jay's chest and escaped as laughter.

"You know, you call me that a lot. How about I give you the whole speech tonight over supper."

He dropped his arms and picked up his things. Immediately, she wanted to be in his embrace, to feel his lips on hers again. "Supper?"

"Yes, I said supper. For now, we'd better get back into the conference if you don't want to miss the rest of it."

"You know what? The conference is the last thing on my mind."

"Hmmmm, sounds interesting. What do you suggest?"

"Well, you forgot to get your things out of my room."

"Oh, I see." He stepped closer to her and put an arm around her waist. "Your room? I think it's my room, but you have the only key that works in the door."

"Let's see, what is the name of your last book? Unwanted Guest, I think."

"You are not unwanted."

The sound of desire in his voice made a chill run up her spine, but she was anything but cold. She pulled the room key from her purse, dangled it in front of him, and placed an inviting kiss on his lips. "Then, with no room to spare, I guess we'll have to share A Roll in the Hay."

SOMETIMES IT'S NOT FOREVER

Clari Potter kicked the golden leaves at her feet as she strolled through the park-like yard of the mansion that was now hers. In her eyes, the future was bleak, but everyone else thought she had it made. The words her mother had said just after Jake's funeral came to mind for the umpteenth time.

"Stop whining. Look what he left you. You can get a bundle out of this place. And there's no telling how much money he had in the bank." She patted Clari's hand. "You are a rich woman."

Did everyone think money was the only thing in life that mattered? She didn't care about all of this splendor. She just wondered how she could go on living without Jake. He was her soul mate, and now he was gone. Why? Why did life deal such hands to people in love?

She approached the steps of the grand mansion.

The marble pillars that supported the porch stood like silent giants who told the cold hard truth. She was alone.

Since the day she'd met her true love, she knew that his job as a Pulitzer Prize winning freelance writer could be dangerous. He had a habit of sticking his nose into stories that sometimes, the people involved didn't want the world to know about. But it wasn't a drug cartel or a terrorist that killed him; it was the government of the country he tried to flee. What secret did he know?

Pictures of his tortured body played through her mind. He was thin, so thin. His cheeks drawn, he barely looked himself. Only the hair she'd run her fingers through so many times, told her Jake was the one inside the coffin. Her husband must have died a terrible death.

No! No, she wouldn't let herself think about the gory details any longer. It was time to move on. Time to start her life again.

Straightening her spine, she took the stairs with a newfound confidence. Jake loved her, and she knew he wouldn't want her pining away any longer. After all, it had been a year since she'd laid him to rest.

The knobs of the double doors that led into the house were cool to the touch. The crisp fall air seemed to follow her into the foyer as she greeted the housekeeper she'd grown so fond of. "Good morning, Bess."

"Morning, ma'am."

A bright smile lit the older woman's face. It had been months since Bess had even lifted the corners of her mouth in a grin. Clari knew she'd loved Jake just like a son and had taken his passing very hard. But this morning there was something about the way Bess carried herself that was different.

"Bess?" She found the matron's mood contagious and was unable to stop the smile that crossed her own face. "What are you up to?"

"Someone in the study to see you, ma'am."

Who in the world would be there at that early hour of the morning? She stepped into the room that had been Jake's favorite, and greeted the man that had so often been there for her since Jake's passing. "Hi, Brian." He turned to face her and took her hands in his. She'd grown accustomed to their comfortable relationship but wondered what brought the man who'd been Jake's partner, here today.

"Clari?"

What was that gleam in his eye? "Yes?"

"I'm the man who's going to make your life complete once again." He squeezed her hands. "But, you have to trust me completely. Can you do that?"

Being with Jake was the only thing that would achieve that miracle for her and that was impossible, but he had always trusted Brian, and she had no reason not to. "Yes," she answered.

* * *

Clari's heart jumped into her throat when the tires screeched against the runway pavement of the tiny airport. She had safely arrived at her destination, and in a few minutes she'd be in the arms of her new man.

She never thought she'd be happy again, but next to the day she married Jake, this was the happiest day of her life.

The small aircraft pulled to a stop, and in moments the pilot opened her door.

"Mrs. Barnell, I'll bring your things shortly. Barney's waitin' for ya."

Barney, how funny, she'd have to get used to that. Butterflies flitted in her stomach at the thought of seeing the man of her dreams again. Their new life together would start when she stepped off the plane.

Her feet hit the ground and there he was. His dark hair shone in the sunlight, and she longed to touch it as she had so many times before. His mesmerizing brown eyes pierced her soul and she knew she'd made the right decision. Her voice escaped just above a whisper, "Barney."

His arms encircled her in a familiar caress of love. An embrace she'd ached for over the last twelve months. His warm breath fanned her cheek and his deep voice murmured softly in her ear.

"I love you."

How she'd longed to hear those simple words again. Tears welled in her eyes. They were alone now, and she could allow his real name to pass quietly through her lips, so only he would hear. "I love you, too, Jake."

REVAMPED

$\mathcal{S}$hannon followed the real estate agent, Hayley, up the stairs to the door of the old frame building. It was just what she'd been looking for. She had always wanted to live in a small town, and right in the middle of the Jonesville Township was the ideal place for her Antique shop.

"Oh, and there's an added bonus to this property," Hayley said, "the river runs just behind the building and there's a great view out the back."

"That sounds wonderful." The peacefulness would surely heal the scars on her heart. It had been almost a year since her husband's fatal car accident, but living in the home they'd shared had been too much of a reminder of his abuse. He had said he loved her, but if that was love, she wanted no part of it. The words I love you were empty and meaningless to her now.

No one knew of his cruelty toward her and she'd vowed to keep it to herself, especially now that he was dead. Even though she still cherished Austin, Texas, the move would be the best thing for her.

She studied the structure. It had been well cared for and the huge windows in front would be just right for her displays. She watched the agent place the key in the wooden framed door that held an old piece of stained glass in its center. She loved the place already and hadn't even been inside.

Hayley pushed the door open and a sound of the tiny bell that hung above the doorway drew Shannon's attention. She shivered and rubbed her arm surprised that goose bumps had risen. How odd. She glanced at the bell and determined it belonged right where it was, and if she decided to buy the property, it would keep its place.

"I see you're admiring the door bell, Miss Rhea."

"Yes, it actually gave me cold chills when I heard its sweet chime. It's beautiful."

The woman smiled and walked to the center of the main room. "Dane has been here since the original owner hung him in that spot over a hundred years ago."

"Oh?" Shannon inhaled as deep as she could to take in all of the scents in the space around her. The musty smell of old, the aroma of cedar, and a faint hint of perfume or cologne filled the air. But the bell, she couldn't get the sound out of her head. "Why do you call the bell, Dane?"

"That's his name."

"Let me get this right. It's a boy bell with the name, Dane." She thought it silly the thing had a name, but she wanted to hear the story behind it.

"Yep."

She brought her gaze back to the tarnished brass object. "Tell me about it, please."

"Well, this building was built and owned by some folks from England. They were a middle aged couple who had been successful in their country, but wanted to see if bigger and better things awaited them in the U.S. They brought their life savings to build and run their shop."

Fascinated by the history of the building, and even the story of the couple, she listened while she walked around the room checking the built in shelving in the walls. "What kind of shop did they have?"

"They had things imported from their homeland and made this an Old English market. Dane belonged to the woman's grandmother who was from Denmark.

"What were the original owners' names?"

"Clifford and Willena." The woman hesitated. "Oh, my gosh!"

Shannon turned toward Hayley. "What? What's wrong?"

Hayley rubbed her arms. "Now I have goose bumps."

"Why?" It got cold all of a sudden. Maybe not cold, but the air was definitely cooler. What was going on?

"Cliff and Willie, their last name was Rhea, spelled exactly like yours."

Her heart skipped a beat. "Rhea?"

"Yes."

Could it be that fate had led her to a building her deceased husband's ancestors built? Why? Now she wished she'd paid more attention to his family history. "Those names don't ring a bell." She glanced at Hayley and started to laugh which echoed throughout the empty building as if to multiply in intensity. Apparently, Hayley hadn't noticed the strange resonance of the laughter as it faded.

The agent walked to the door. "They don't ring a bell, huh. No pun intended, right?"

Dane released his musical sound again with the door closing and this time it warmed her instead of making her shiver. Almost like it welcomed her, but how could that be? It was a bell for heaven sake. Now her imagination was getting the best of her.

"No pun, trust me." She might do some research on his family tree. It was intriguing to think his relatives could have built this. "Now, tell me more about Dane." Calling a door bell by name, it was madness! But it felt natural.

"Dane is a good luck piece and once he was mounted, he's never been moved. On Cliff and Willena's wedding day in the 1850's, Willena's grandmother gave the bell to her so it would ring her granddaughter a prosperous life. It worked, and when the Rheas moved here, they named the bell Dane, which means, from Denmark… like Willie's grandma was."

"Wow, that's so interesting." She met the red haired agent's gaze. "How come you know so much about this place?"

"I've lived in Jonesville all my life. My mother

is from here originally and after she and Dad married, they stayed.

"My father, Ben Jones, was the township's historian. He worked in this building when he was a young man, so did my brother. It was an antique shop then, too. Come to think of it, since the Rheas have been gone, it's always been an antique shop.

"However, it's been empty for some time now. The township has maintained it pretty well."

Shannon studied the shiny hardwood floors and clean interior of the shop. "Yes, I'd say someone has. May I ask why it's been empty?"

Hayley chuckled. "It's silly, but some say that after Willena passed away, Clifford felt her presence here and now that he's gone, it's thought that they are both here in spirit."

Haunted? She swallowed hard and thought of the sudden change she'd felt in the air earlier. In all of her twenty six years, she'd never believed in ghosts, and she wasn't going to start now. However, it fascinated her. "You're right, that is silly."

Stepping toward a closed door, Hayley said, "I agree, now would you like to see the apartment up stairs?"

"Yes, I love the idea of living above the shop. So far, I couldn't have built a place more suited for me if I'd done it myself."

"I'm glad to hear it." Hayley opened the door and led the way up the stairs.

All Shannon could think of, was how would she ever get her furniture up there? "These are so narrow."

"There's an outside stairway, too. It leads to the

main entrance of the apartment. I think you'll like it. There's a beautiful deck that was added on a few years ago, so you can walk out your front door and look right at the river. It's really peaceful out there. Now, this door opens into the kitchen," she said as she opened the door at the top of the stairs.

Shannon liked the thought of having a door at the bottom and top of the stairs. That made the apartment more private in a way. She entered the small kitchen and instantly fell in love. "This is so cute." Even though it was empty, she imagined her belongings placed around the area.

Glass front cabinets lined the walls and light colored counter tops lay beneath. The refrigerator wasn't full sized, but she didn't need anything bigger, and the undersized four burner gas stove fit neatly in its cubby hole. "How adorable, I love it."

"Wait till you see the rest."

When they entered the living area, she knew she was home. A large picture window allowed the sun to brighten the room and when she looked out, the river ran less than 100 feet away. Wild honeysuckle climbed the trunks of towering oak trees. She opened the door that led to the large wooden deck and inhaled the sweet aroma. Her decision was made. "I'll take it."

"But you haven't even seen the oversized claw-foot bathtub yet."

"Claw-foot bathtub?   Now I know I'm in heaven. Let's get on with the paper work. I'm ready to move in and get my business started." Dane rang from the floor below, or was she hearing things? "Did you hear that?" she asked Hayley.

"What?"

"Dane."

"No."

"Well, I think someone just came in downstairs." She went to the stairway and headed down with Hayley behind her switching off lights on the way.

Upon entry of the main room of the shop, all was quiet. Why had she thought she'd heard the doorbell ring? Was it her imagination again? Was this place really haunted? No. She glanced up at Dane and he slightly swayed back and forth. Surely the bell hadn't rung by itself.

"What was that?" Hayley asked.

Shannon jumped and her heart threatened to burst out of her chest. "What the...?" She turned toward the direction where the door had slammed. To her surprise, a man stood behind them. Was he a ghost?

CHAPTER 2

*H*ayley put her hand to her chest. "Cary, what are you doing here? You scared the hell out of us?"

"Sorry, I was just double checking the work I did in the store room. I saw your car and knew the door would be unlocked, so I came on in."

The man stood at least six foot three. He was distinguished looking with his slightly graying, sandy brown hair. It had been a long time since Shannon had seen someone with a flattop haircut, but he wore it well.

He looked familiar. Did she know him? She stepped toward him and admired his muscular frame. His jeans didn't fit too badly either. "Hi, I'm Shannon." She offered him a handshake.

The man accepted her gesture. "Cary, ma'am, Cary Jones."

Heat rushed up her arm, through her veins and to her very core, but she didn't let go of his grasp, nor did she want to. "Have we met somewhere? I sense that I know you." A strange feeling bubbled up inside her. Who was this man? His smile didn't hide the unsure look in his beautiful green eyes.

"I get the same feeling, but I can't think of where it might have been."

"Well, it's nice to meet you." He held her hand just a little too long, but she still couldn't pull away. The skin tingled where he touched it, and the scent of cologne she'd admired earlier was now more present in the air. Damn he smelled good. She gazed into his eyes and saw kindness there. Familiarity? But that wasn't logical. When released his grasp on her hand she shivered missing the warmth of his touch.

Cary put his arm around Hayley's waist when she stepped up next to him. "How are you doing, babe?" he asked.

"Great now that you're here." Hayley stood on her toes and gave Cary a peck on the cheek.

It was clear that Hayley and Cary were close. The look in the other woman's eyes showed she had high admiration for Cary, maybe even love. She felt ridiculous for having such an immediate attraction to the man when it was obvious he and Hayley was a couple.

Hayley's attention once again came back to Shannon. "Cary is the mayor of our township."

"Mayor, I'm impressed." Actually, she was more than impressed with his status as mayor; she was totally impressed with him, and understood why Hayley was so enamored. She, however, should have no interest, not after what she'd lived through the last couple of years of her marriage. She had to remember that a man in her life was the last thing she wanted, or needed.

Cary smiled. "Well, don't be too impressed, I don't really have to do anything, our town almost runs itself, I just wear the name. I make my living doing carpentry, building furniture and collecting and restoring antique pieces. Are you thinking about joining our little community?"

"Yes. I think I will."

"So you're buying this old haunted shop?" he asked with a chuckle.

Somehow it seemed like he belonged in the building. The way he looked at the structure made it clear he loved it. "I believe I will buy it, Mr. Jones, but I don't believe in hauntings."

"Please, call me Cary." He dropped his arm from Hayley's waist. "That's good to know. It will be nice to have a new, beautiful face in Jonesville."

What did he think was so good to know? That she was joining the community or that she didn't believe in hauntings. She didn't care, besides, was he flirting with her? How rude, and right in front of his girlfriend. Maybe she just thought she was impressed with him.

Then why, if she didn't approve of his actions, did he cause her heartbeat to run away with itself. His smile showed straight white teeth and a warm breeze seemed to pass between them when he stepped closer. Another temperature change, how weird.

"What are you going to do with this wonderful old place?"

She met his gaze. Suddenly, the warmth

overwhelmed her and she was uncomfortable in his presence. Not really uncomfortable, maybe, comfortable? Whatever, she didn't know what it was but something wasn't right.

The air seemed statically charged between her and the man in front of her. She took a step back, but an unknown entity pulled her closer. It wasn't a physical pull, more like something inside her. An emotion she'd never felt before.

A lump formed in her throat so she swallowed hard and forced back the feelings. Maybe it was simply because she thought he was attractive. That had to be it. Anything else was unacceptable. He belonged to Hayley.

She thought back to the question of what she was going to do with the building. "My husband and I owned an antique shop in Austin." She had always loved antiques, her husband, on the other hand, never had and blamed her for every little thing that went wrong.

He had been the one who wanted to own a business. It wasn't her fault he'd insisted on opening the shop. But he'd known if it was something she loved, like antiquing, she would do all of the work, and she did. So it was her fault for allowing him to use her that way. At least it kept her busy and away from him part of the time. She had to stop thinking about it, it was over.

The real estate agent smiled. "Husband? You didn't tell me you're married."

She wouldn't have been surprised to hear a slight bit of relief in the other woman's voice. "No, Hayley, I didn't because I'm not, I'm a widow."

"My condolences." Hayley paused. "Then, that would mean Rhea is your married name?"

"Yes. My maiden name is Kirby. I was going to take it back when Peter was killed, but for some reason I changed my mind."

"Killed? Oh, that's awful."

"Time's making the pain better. It's been almost a year since it happened. After the car wreck, I closed the store. Now I feel I should move on." She glanced around the room that seemed so familiar. What had drawn her to this small community? "I still have most of my inventory. I love antiquing and this will be a great shop."

Cary said, "I'm sorry about your husband, but I assure you, you'll love it in our little town of five-hundred."

"Wow, five-hundred." His voice was deep, smooth and it soothed her in a way, but she couldn't bring herself to look him in the eye again. "That would add up to one subdivision in Austin." She was pleased when they both laughed. She wasn't sure, but she hoped she'd get out of there with little or no more uneasiness, or whatever it was she experienced in Cary Jones' presence.

If her first encounter in the small community, with a person other than Hayley, made her have feelings entirely alien to her, maybe she'd been too hasty in her decision.

Hayley stepped toward the door, her laughter subsiding. "But, Shannon, a subdivision in Austin doesn't have the character Jonesville Township does."

"You're right about that." She took a quick

look around the room one more time, then thought about the small apartment above. She couldn't allow a womanizer like Cary Jones to dissuade her decision. However she would do some soul searching to find out why she was even attracted to the man when he was spoken for.

She glanced around the empty room once again. No, this was home. She belonged here. One thing she now knew for sure was that the Rhea Building would belong to her.

Cary reached for the door knob. "Maybe we can get together soon." He met Shannon's gaze.

Get together? How dare he ask her out right in front of Hayley? If nothing else his arrogance should help her fight any feelings she could develop for him if he were available. "I doubt it. I'll be very busy getting settled." He smiled that perfect smile and she found herself lost in his gaze. Why did she feel like she knew him?

"Maybe after you get settled, I can come in and see if you need some pieces refurbished."

She had to break the spell he was casting on her. "Thank you, Mr. Jones, but I do my own restoration."

"Cary, Shannon and I better get going to the office," Hayley said. "We have a lot of paper work to do.

"Okay." He opened the door. "Will I see you at the house later?"

"Yeah, about six."

"You know what to bring."

Shannon was almost embarrassed to hear the personal conversation between lovers. Especially, after he'd tried to make a date with her. At the same time, she felt the pangs of jealousy stab at her heart. She watched Cary bend and give Hayley a hug and a loving kiss on the forehead then heard the woman's words.

"Only for you, my darling, only for you."

CHAPTER 3

Cary drove toward home and couldn't stop thinking about the woman named Shannon. Her long blond hair had been fashioned in a soft braid down her back and short tendrils wisped around her face. Her blue eyes sparkled in the sunlight that filtered through the big windows of the old building, and her hand was as soft as velvet when he clasped it in his.

The uncanny notion that they'd met before still lingered in his mind. Wracking his brain, he couldn't figure out why he knew her, but he did. Next time he saw her, maybe it would ignite a spark of recollection as to where they'd met.

He understood why she wouldn't accept his offer to get together. She probably had misunderstood what he'd meant. He wasn't actually proposing a date, was he? No, his offer was for companionship since she didn't know anyone in Jonesville, but it was probably too soon after her husband's passing for her to consider it.

How stupid of him not to think about that before he asked, but even if she didn't want to go out, he'd thought surely she'd be interested in doing business with him. Oh, well, nothing he could do about it now. He only hoped that the old Rhea building didn't get to her as it had to everyone else who'd ever owned it besides Cliff and Willie.

It had sat empty for many years before the last tenants took it about ten years earlier. They kept it the longest, but still, they left a couple of years ago. It was a beautiful old building and added so much to their little township, but the things that happened there were too much for folks to stand.

Why had he never experienced any of the hauntings? He'd been in there for hours by himself and felt nothing but comforted. At home really, but that wouldn't happen now. His thoughts to buy the old building and open his own shop were swept under the rug by the new girl in town. His pulse quickened at the thought of the warmth her touch spread through his body. How could a mere stranger have that effect on him? Was she a stranger?

Taking a deep breath, he pulled into the parking lot of Franklin's. A cold drink sounded like the perfect thing to wet his whistle.

He studied the outside of the establishment, then glanced up and down the main street. He loved this little town. Even after he'd moved to the city, he longed to come home. Something drew him to the small community, and it was an easy decision for him to come back to help take care of his mother. After his father died, it was too much for his sister to take care of the house, their mom and work at the same time.

"Hi, Cary, want your regular root beer float today?" the waitress asked.

"No, Cassie, I think I'll just have a root beer, no ice cream."

"Are you on a diet or somethin'?" She glanced at him and chuckled.

"Just big plans for supper tonight and I want to leave room."

"Oh, I see."

He watched her set the bubbling brown liquid on the counter and put a straw in it. "Hey, Cass, your grandpa here?"

"Yep, he's cooking today. Want me to go get him?"

Cary glanced around the obviously empty room and smiled. "If he's not busy."

She laughed. "You came in at just the right time," she said, as she went into the kitchen.

He sipped on his soda and admired the nostalgic soda fountain setting. It had been the same for the last sixty or more years. Even the old hanging lights were original and well cared for.

It pleased him to know the residents of Jonesville took pride in the appearance of the township. It helped to bring tourists in during the summer season. It was a treat to the visitors to be able to shop at the quaint businesses and float the river, too.

The older man entered the room wiping his hands on a crisp, clean white apron. Johnny Franklin had been Cary's dad's best friend and he found himself turning to Johnny for advice more times than not. "Hey, you old fart. You run everyone off with that grouchy attitude of yours?"

"Old fart? You watch your manners young man. I can still take you out behind the shed." He took a seat on a barstool.

Cary sniggered. He loved the old man. "It wouldn't be the first time, but I bet I can out run you now."

"Don't be smart. What brings you here today? No doubt you're seeking my advice because of my abundant wisdom."

"You are big-headed aren't you, ol' man? Matter of fact, I brought news."

"Oh, probably something I already know."

"That Hayley's going to sell the Rhea building to a beautiful young lady? Did you know that?" He could tell he'd peaked Johnny's interest, and concerns. He met the man's gaze and nodded.

"Hmmmmm, interesting. We'd better get a booth and talk about this." Johnny got off his stool. "Cassie, would you bring me a cup of coffee, please?"

"Sure, Papa John."

Cary picked up his root beer and followed John to the booth. "I know what you're thinking."

"Damn right. That place should be torn down. Too many weird things happen in there. I'll put a hundred on the table she won't stay through tourist season."

He thought about Shannon and the strength in her beautiful blue eyes. Besides, she said she didn't believe in ghosts. What the hell. "Okay, old man, you're on." Just the thought of tearing down the building made his blood run cold. It was a historical mark in Jonesville and he loved it.

John took his coffee cup from his granddaughter. "Thanks, baby girl."

"Welcome," she replied and walked away.

"Who is this woman?"

"An antique dealer from Austin."

John shook his head. "Another antique shop going in there. Does she know it's haunted?"

"Yep, and she still wants it. You know, I've been in there many times and have never had any encounters."

"You're too all fired mean for any ghost to want to mess with you."

"Hey, now, that's not fair." The soda tingled on its way down, then he placed his glass back on the table. Ice clanked against the glass as he moved the brown liquid around with his straw, knowing full well it didn't need stirring. "Actually, she said she doesn't believe in ghosts."

"That'll change. Does she know that both Clifford and his wife died in that apartment?"

"I'm not sure about that. I'll ask Hayley tonight when she comes over."

"She'd better be totally up front with the lady before they sign any papers. I'd hate for the woman to have to sell out and run like the others have."

It was true; Shannon deserved to know all of the details about the haunting, or whatever it was. "You're right. I'll call and tell Hayley that." He reached for his cell phone and pressed Hayley's quick dial number. One thing he couldn't stand the thought of was losing Shannon, the woman he loved. What the hell? Where had that come from?

CHAPTER 4

"*H*ello?"

Shannon tried not to pay attention to Hayley's phone conversation as she studied the documents in front of her. She only hoped the owners took her offer. It was at the low end of what she could afford, so if they made her a counter offer, she'd be in the position to counter again if needed.

"No, not yet, but we're about to make an offer....Why? I didn't think about it....I guess you're right....Yes, I'll do it now....Okay....I love you, too, see you tonight.... Bye."

She couldn't help but hear what Hayley was saying so she assumed she'd been talking to Cary Jones. She thought back to his bright smile and kind eyes and her heart skipped a beat. He was all she'd ever wanted, but how could she know that, she'd only seen him one time. So, why did she feel like she knew him?

What was wrong with her and what was she

doing thinking about him when she was doing business with his sweetheart? You must be losing your mind! She had to shake the memory and get on with the deal. "Do you think they'll take this offer?"

"It would be nice if they did."

Hayley fidgeted and squirmed in her seat. Shannon was puzzled by the look on the woman's face. Apparently the phone conversation had been about her buying the building and she felt she had the right to ask. "Was that your boyfriend? Is something wrong?"

Sitting back in her chair, the agent said, "My boyfriend? No, that was Cary."

"Well, I thought…"

The woman began to laugh. "You thought Cary was my boyfriend? That's hilarious," she stated between guffaws.

Now Shannon was totally confused, but the other woman's amusement was contagious. It seemed like such a long time since she'd really let go and laughed but now it came easy.

She finally caught her breath. "Boy, that felt good, but why is that funny? I mean, at the shop he kissed you and told you he loved you. And don't you two have a date for supper tonight?"

Hayley wiped tears from her eyes. "Yes, I guess I can see where you might think that, but Cary is not my lover, he's my brother. Our date is at our mother's house. Cary helps me take care of her and every Saturday night we get together at her place for supper. Cary's a great cook."

Shannon's heart leapt in her chest and her stomach did flip flops. They weren't lovers!

Thinking back on the encounter, she couldn't figure out why she'd read more into it than was there. Was she trying to protect her own heart? "Your brother? Boy, I feel like an idiot." At least now she didn't have so much guilt about the thoughts and feelings she'd been experiencing.

Shaking her head Hayley said, "Don't, there was no way you could have known. Cary's the most single man I know and he's going to laugh his butt off when he hears this."

"You don't have to tell him."

"Oh, yes I do, this is classic. Just like your little shop's going to be, Shannon."

Now that she thought about it, it would be nice for him to know because he might ask her to 'get together soon', again in the future. She found herself truly smiling about both Cary being single, and making the offer on the shop.

"Maybe we'd better move on with making the offer." Again she noticed the concerned look on the agent's face, and she remembered the phone conversation the woman had had with her brother. "Is there something about the deal you're not telling me?"

"No, not exactly." Hayley hesitated. "Well, kind of. I guess before we make your offer, you need to know a little more about the haunting at the Rhea building."

It sounded funny to hear Hayley call the property 'The Rhea Building', but she loved the sound of it almost as much as she loved the building itself. However she was troubled that the alleged haunting had become more of an issue. "What about it? I told you I don't believe in ghosts."

"My brother," Hayley said and smiled, "thought you should know the full story behind it before you make your final decision."

At least Shannon knew Cary was thinking about her. Could he really be interested? Why was she allowing herself to imagine these things? It didn't matter if he was interested or not, she wasn't, or at least she didn't want to permit herself to be. But with Cary it was hard; there was something about him that made her want to know him. Every inch of him. "That was nice of your brother. Go ahead, tell me more."

"It may not make any difference to you, but both Cliff and Willie died on the premises, actually, in the bedroom of the apartment."

"No, that doesn't bother me in the least. People died at home in those days." Then why did she feel a sudden sadness?

"At times, after Willena passed, patrons would catch Cliff talking to himself. He claimed he was talking to Willie."

Shannon didn't think that was so unusual. "I have to admit that after my husband was killed, I spoke to him sometimes, but I didn't think he was actually there."

Hayley sat back in her chair. "Well, the difference is, Cliff thought his wife's spirit was with him all of the time. He professed he could see her now and again.

"After Cliff died, the second owners couldn't handle the fact that they would hear a man's voice in the building when no one else was there. Then items in the shop would get moved from one place to another, or disappear altogether.

"They decided to sell when the wife thought she saw the figure of a woman standing over her in the bedroom. When she got up, the apparition was gone."

Unable to believe what she was hearing, she began to laugh. "That's the most ridiculous thing I've ever heard. Ghosts standing over the bed, things disappearing because a ghost took them, it's crazy."

"Not big things disappeared," Hayley continued, "just small items, but all were valuable pieces from England. Most had belonged to Cliff and Willie and somehow found their way back to the shop only to mysteriously vanish."

Shannon didn't know why they were even having this conversation? "You know as well as I do, Hayley, that those things most likely walked out the door with some customer that was too cheap to pay for them."

"I have to admit you're probably right, but that's not all. After those folks sold out, the next few owners missed items and heard the voices, too. Dane would ring in the middle of the night. It seemed he held a key of some sort, because if they heard him in the night, they knew something would be missing, or moved, in the morning."

"Well, there you go; someone was coming in and taking it."

"No, no one was there. Many times they would go immediately and check. The door was locked and no one was inside."

Thinking about what the woman had said, Shannon came to a conclusion. "There has to be a logical explanation for these things happening. Did anyone ever find any of the stolen items?"

"Not a trace."

"What about the folks I'm buying the building from. Were they scared away, too?"

"Not frightened away, no. The folks you're buying the property from didn't let a lot of that bother them. Actually, they didn't have much haunting after they moved in. It just so happened they were from England, too. We all wondered if that made a difference to Cliff and Willie. The Crawford's stayed a few years."

Surely Hayley didn't believe in the haunting, but from what she had just said, she did. Shannon reminded herself that she didn't believe in such things, so nothing like that would happen to her, but now her curiosity was peaked. "So, why did they leave?"

Hayley sat forward and put her elbows on the table. "As I told you, the Rhea building has always, for some reason, been an antique shop.

"The Crawford's had gone to Dallas to an auction. They bought a box of goods, but didn't see all of the individual items that were included. You know how auctions are when they sell in bulk to liquidate."

Shannon knew exactly what she was talking about. She'd bought bulk at auctions before.

"Anyway, after the couple got back to the shop and began to go through what they'd purchased. They found a small wooden box, and inside it, wrapped in a silk cloth was an old set of gold wedding bands. They were thrilled."

"Yes, I would have been too."

"They figured the set dated back to the mid eighteen hundreds. With further inspection they studied the rings with magnifying glass and what they found engraved inside the bands astonished them, and everyone in Jonesville."

Enthralled with Hayley's story, Shannon hadn't, until now, noticed she was sitting on the edge of her chair. What was the woman waiting for? "Come on, tell me. What was engraved on them?"

Hayley cleared her throat as if it was hard for her to say the words. Tears welled in her eyes and Shannon felt sudden warmth around her. "Don't keep me in suspense, Hayley. What did the rings say?" The warmth turned to a chill and she shivered.

The agent inhaled deeply then exhaled. "Clifford and Willena."

She hadn't realized she'd been holding her breath until she released the air in her lungs and sat back in her chair. "What?"

"Yes, they were the Rhea's wedding bands."

"What a coincidence. Why would that make the Crawfords leave?"

"That's not what did it; they placed the rings in the same glass cabinet that's still in the building."

"The one against that back wall?"

"Yes, it belonged to the Rhea's originally. That old display case was where they locked the bands up and showcased them, with no intentions of selling the pair. It was like an historical event here in town. Everyone was so thrilled that part of Clifford and Willena was back, they flooded the shop admiring the rings. After about three weeks on display, the gold bands disappeared."

Why would someone do something like that? It was beyond her how some people had no conscience. "How did it happen? You said the case was locked, didn't you?"

Hayley nodded, "It was, with the original lock the Rhea's had used. It is very old and there is only one key. The lock stays with the case. It's in the shop right now."

Shannon swallowed the lump in her throat as she watched the woman walk across the room to a little safe. Hayley opened the secure box and took out a small satin bag. The moment she shut the door to the lock box, Shannon noticed a musty smell in the air. What was it?

She knew exactly what it was. The feeling she had when the other woman handed her the satin bag was something she'd never experienced. The key, somehow she felt it belonged to her. Why did she feel it something she'd had forever and she'd missed it? She closed her fingers around the soft holder and felt the metal object inside. "Thank you for giving this back to me." The look on Hayley's face made her realize what she'd said.

"Pardon me?"

What was happening? None of this made sense. "I-I don't know why I said that." She saw Hayley shiver.

"I don't either, but for a minute it gave me the creeps."

"Finish your story, please." She glanced down at the hand that held the key. Why hadn't she realized she was grasping it so tightly? Her knuckles were white from the pressure. She opened the bag, removed the key and put it on the desk top. It looked brand new.

Hayley sat in her chair once again. "No one could comprehend how the rings had vanished into thin air. There was no evidence someone had been in the cabinet, or the shop. The rings were just gone."

She couldn't believe it. "Did the officials dust for fingerprints?"

"Yes, nothing."

"How bizarre." Could it be that all of these peculiar things actually happened because of a haunting? No, that was ridiculous and she refused to allow herself to think about it. Even though her personal experiences so far had been, in the least, different and the way the key felt in her– No!

"Yes, bizarre. Now you see why we thought you should know everything. The Crawfords decided that was the last straw. They were like you and figured someone local was stealing from them so they are selling out."

"May I ask how long they have been gone?"

"About two years. They left just before my father passed away." The woman cleared her throat. "Now, if you change your mind, I'll understand."

Shannon nodded; she would definitely have to think about this now. However, what was there to think about? She loved the place. It was exactly what she'd been looking for and all she had to do was install cameras. If someone secretly got into the shop, she'd have them on video and the mystery would be solved.

Smiling at Hayley she said, "I'm not changing my mind because there's a thief around. Hopefully, they got what they wanted and won't come back to the scene of the crime. Let's make that offer."

She picked up the key and returned it to its satin bag. It was all she could do to force herself to hand it back to Hayley. It wasn't hers and logic told her it never had been, but somehow she felt it had. She would have to be satisfied to know that if the deal went through, the key would be hers again.

CHAPTER 5

Cary enjoyed having the top down on his classic nineteen fifty seven Ford Fairlane. His Saturday afternoon drive brought him into town to pick up some things for his mother, but all he could do was think about Shannon Rhea.

As he passed by the Rhea building, he glanced at the store front. Shannon had named her new antique shop Revamped and the new sign was hung. The windows were again full of displays he thought very tastefully done. She was not only beautiful, by the looks of the designs, she was talented as well.

It had been a month since she opened her doors and, even though it seemed something drew him to the place, he hadn't been inside yet. As hard as it was, he'd forced himself to stay away.

The more he'd thought about the old Jonesville Township's historic Rhea Building, the more he realized he'd always been particularly fond of it. Even as a boy he'd loved it and his first job had been working for one of the previous owners. That's where he'd learned so much about antiques, though it seemed the knowledge came naturally.

When he'd been renovating parts of the structure before Shannon bought it, he noticed how comfortable he felt. He would love to visit her now and see what she'd done to the inside. He wouldn't mind seeing the prettiest woman in town, either. However, invading Shannon's privacy was something he didn't want to do.

Amusing as it was that she thought he and Hayley were lovers, she'd made it clear she wasn't interested in him, or any man for that matter. He decided to give her enough time to settle in before he went to see her new business and officially welcome her to Jonesville.

The few times they had seen each other, which was inevitable in the small township, he'd thought the meetings were friendly. Though he'd said cordial hellos and gone about his business, the strings of his heart tugged a tighter grip of interest in the woman. Something he'd never felt before. It was more or less like he'd always known her and maybe even... loved her.

Wanting to get involved with a woman after his last attempt miserably failed, was something he didn't think he'd do for a long time. There'd been something missing with every woman he'd dated, but Shannon Rhea was different, there was something about her that intrigued him.

She was so young to be a widow and must have been very in love with her husband. He figured it would take her awhile to get over her loss, however, every time their gaze met, a spark ignited between them. No, not just a spark but a force that bonded them in some way, he couldn't figure it out, but found himself wanting to pursue a relationship with her.

Thoughts of blond tendrils framing her face and big blue eyes gazing up at him entered his mind. He glanced in his rear view mirror and watched the shop growing smaller in the reflection. "Oh, the hell with it!" He turned his car around and parked directly in front of Revamped.

Now was as good of a time as any to greet her. Why was he putting it off, and why was he making excuses to do so?

He felt like a high school boy afraid to ask a girl to the prom. He had to keep it in his mind that all he wanted to do was welcome her to town. It was his job as mayor.

That wasn't the reason at all. Even with all of his inner turmoil about the situation, his past girlfriends, and Shannon's recent loss, he still wanted to spend time with her.

Dane jingled when he opened the door and stepped inside the small shop. His heart skipped a beat when he saw Shannon working on a display across the room. How could he feel like he was in love with a woman he didn't even know? He swallowed hard, surprised at how nervous he truly was. "Hi."

Shannon jumped when she heard a man's voice and turned toward the sound. "Cary." She felt awkward for some reason, but at the same time exhilarated that he was there. She'd been wondering when he was going to visit, but she didn't know butterflies would invade her stomach when he did.

Why hadn't Dane warned her someone had entered? She pushed strands of hair away from her face, toward her braid. "I didn't hear you come in."

"Sorry if I startled you." He glanced around the shop. "The place looks great! You've got some really nice pieces."

His smile made her tingle inside. She walked toward him and offered a handshake when she really wanted to put her arms around his neck and kiss him. "Thanks."

He grasped her hand. "It's good to see you."

The static in the air made the hair on back of Shannon's neck stand up. Why did this happen every time she got close to this man? But most of all, did he notice it? She realized he did when he quickly withdrew his hand.

"It's good to see you, too." She hadn't realized until that moment that she'd missed him. Why did she feel as if Cary was a loved one who had finally returned home from a journey?

It was hard to tear her gaze from his, oh so memorable, eyes. She felt she knew them by heart and had looked into their depths for a life time. What was it about him that made him so familiar? She forced herself to look away. "Well, er... come on in and look around."

He turned and strolled through the store, studying its contents. "How've things been going?"

"So far, so good." Better now that he was there, but she wouldn't tell him that. "I love my little shop. It feels like home."

"No weird encounters? Nothing coming up missing or anything?"

She chuckled. "No, not yet, but I was wondering why Dane didn't ring when you came in."

Cary glanced her way. "He did."

"He did? Well, I didn't hear him, and I usually hear him every time the door opens. So, I guess that's the first weird thing that's happened." She enjoyed hearing Cary laugh.

"I see you put the Rhea's display case back in its original spot. I'm glad Hayley told you where it went."

Shannon shook her head. "No one told me to put it there, that's where it belongs." Cary rubbed his hand along the edge of the glass, but what she saw in his eyes was more than admiration. "It's a beautiful piece of furniture isn't it?"

Cary nodded. "Yes, I've always loved it, and you're right, it belongs right here." He met her gaze. "So do you."

Heat of passion blazed in his eyes. Why did she feel like she'd been there before? She placed her fingertips to her lips when the warmth of a kiss brushed against them, but Cary hadn't kissed her. Her mind was playing tricks she didn't understand.

This time, she couldn't force herself to look away from his mesmerizing green eyes. He stepped closer. Close enough the heat of his body penetrated her clothing. Then he took her in his arms and she didn't object because it felt right, natural. But how could she know that?

"Shannon, I—"

Within a heartbeat he bent and pressed his lips to hers. Everything faded around them and her world was in this man's embrace, his kiss. Was it her heart she felt beating or his? It was as if they were one, and had always been.

She didn't want it to end. An unexplained emptiness invaded her when he slowly ended the kiss and stepped away. Passion and longing still evident on his face.

What was wrong with him? The overwhelming desire to kiss the beautiful woman in his arms was more than he could control. The last thing Cary wanted to do was let her go, but he had to. He had no right to overstep his boundaries.

He forced himself to release her lips when all he really wanted was to kiss her longer, deeper, make love to her. It was all he could do to step away from her warmth. He fought to catch his breath. "I-I don't know what came over me. Please forgive me."

The flush of her face made her more beautiful than ever. He loved the way she pushed the loose curls away from her face and wondered what she'd look like if all of her hair hung loose across her shoulders.

"Forgive you?" She turned and walked away. "I don't remember protesting what just happened."

"No, I guess you didn't." He smiled and remembered how she'd leaned into him, welcomed his kiss, even acted like she wanted more. The feel of her breast pressed against his chest caused blood to rush to his groin. He had to leave before he took even more advantage of the situation and kissed her again.

She was facing the window and her hair glistened in the sunlight. He desperately wanted to reach out and touch it. How had this woman captured his heart so quickly? Had she been there all along? Was she the one he'd been waiting for?

He'd known for a long time his soul mate was out there somewhere. Now she was here. He felt it to the core of his very being.

He approached her from behind and placed his hands on her shoulders. Her breath caught and he knew she felt the same charge of energy he had.

Dare he turn her around? No, he was having enough trouble controlling his emotions without seeing her beautiful face. "Shannon, I don't know what's happening between us, but you and I both know it's something beyond our control. You feel it, don't you?" The way she nodded her head gave him affirmation.

"I don't want to go, but I need to." He dropped his hands and she turned to face him. Her blue eyes, filled with want and questions.

The warmth of Cary's arms, the feel of his lips, his taste, was everything Shannon knew it would be. "Yes, I think you need to go, too."

She had to compose herself. What was happening between them? Whatever it was she was afraid of it and loved it at the same time. Damn the man for making her love him. Love? That was impossible; she'd seen him all of maybe a dozen times so why did it feel like she'd known him forever? "I appreciate you coming by, though."

Cary stepped toward her and her breath caught in her throat. Was he going to kiss her again? She wanted him to more than anything, but Dane rang out a warning that someone had entered the shop. They backed away from each other and she wondered if they looked like a couple of kids caught with their hands in a cookie jar. She smiled at the thought and glanced at Cary who had a wide grin.

"What are you smiling at?" He asked.

"What are you smiling at?" She couldn't believe it when simultaneously they both said,

"Cookie jar". His laughter filled the room and she couldn't help but join in as she walked beside him toward the door.

"Would you consider having supper with me tonight? I'd love to introduce you to my mother. Hayley will be there, too."

Before she had time to think about it, her heart compelled her to say, "Yes, I'd like that."

"Great! I'll pick you up at six."

"I'll be ready." She opened the door and Dane rang out happily. That was absurd, how could his ring sound any happier then it always did? Watching Cary walk to his car, she struggled with the urge to run after him, but the realization that she'd see him again in a few hours made the need bearable.

CHAPTER 6

*S*hannon glanced at her reflection in the mirror for about the hundredth time. The jeans and white cotton gypsy shirt she'd decided to wear were comfortable, but was it a suitable outfit for supper? Mostly she wondered if it would please Cary.

A knock at the door brought a sudden stop to her observation and made her blood rush with anticipation. She glanced at her watch. Six o'clock on the dot. At least he was punctual.

She walked from the bathroom across the living room to the door. Placing her hand to her throat, she wondered if her heart was going to be right out her chest. The doorknob was cool to the touch, unlike the heat that rushed to her face when she greeted the most handsome man she'd ever seen. "Cary, hi, come in."

"I'd better not; I wouldn't want the enchiladas to burn."

She turned the lock in the knob, stepped onto

the deck, met his gaze and closed the door. "What's that supposed to mean?" His eyes smoldered with suggestion.

"You know full well what it means."

She did and it excited her to think about being in his arms, naked, making love. "Mmmmm, I love the thought… of enchiladas that is."

"So do I, and I'll bet they'll be the best in the state of Texas. I make a mean green sauce. I hope you like chicken, they're my specialty."

"Absolutely love chicken enchiladas! They're my favorite."

"Now, how'd I know that?"

She, too, wondered how they knew so much about each other. Maybe she really didn't know it, but it was in the back of her mind that he loved milk. She shook her head. What a silly thought.

Though it didn't take long for them to get through town, she enjoyed the drive to his mother's home. They rode in comfortable silence.

He pulled onto a long gravel drive then stopped once they passed through the entrance of the property. She watched his muscles flex as he got out and closed the gate.

She was fascinated by the energy that passed between them when they were close to each other. How could being around him seem so natural in such a short time? Was there something unexplainable about the two of them and their pull to each other?

As they moved toward the house she was awed by the surrounding area. They approached from the back side and she could see the home was built into the side of a hill. Both stories were visible from behind, but in front it looked like it was only one floor.

Cary got out, went to her side of the car and opened her door. The sun was still visible over the tall trees of the wooded yard. The smell of lilacs drifted through the air and she was at peace. "This is beautiful."

"Thank you. It belonged to my grandparents. My mother's lived here almost all of her life."

She followed Cary into the house. Once inside the open floor plan allowed her to see into the kitchen. She breathed in the aromas of fresh salsa, green chilies and chili powder. "Wow, if this food tastes as good as it smells, you might be right about it being the best in Texas."

"Hi, Shannon."

Hayley came out of the kitchen wiping her hands on a small towel. She was such a beautiful woman and Shannon loved the color of her hair. Her green eyes were the same color as her brother's, and just as kind. "Hi. It smells great in here." She glanced at the redhead's apron then at Cary. "I thought you said you made the chicken enchiladas."

"He did," his sister said, "I saw y'all drive up so I was just getting things on the table. I'll just finish up while you meet Mom."

Cary took her purse and placed it on the end table next to the couch. "See how quick you are to think I would story to you?" he said.

A lie would never leave his lips. He was the most honest man she knew and she would trust him with her life. There it was again. That uncanny feeling they'd known each other for years.

Shannon heard footsteps from the hallway behind her. She assumed it was Cary and Hayley's mother, so she turned to greet her.

"This is my mother, Pat. Mom, meet Shannon, she bought the old R—"

The smile she'd had faded when she saw the look of shock in the older woman's eyes and the color drain from her face.

"Mother? Are you alright." Cary rushed to his mother's side.

She wouldn't stop staring at Shannon. "I-I need to sit down, that's all."

Cary helped Pat to a chair and Shannon saw that the woman was trembling. She hadn't even said hello to her. Surely she didn't dislike her already.

"What happened?" Hayley rushed to her mother's side. "Mom, you're as white as a sheet. You look like you've just seen a ghost."

Why wouldn't the woman stop staring at her? She wanted to run from the scrutiny, but with further study, she saw no ill feelings in her eyes. But there was something akin to disbelief. Shannon swallowed the lump that had formed in her throat and forced herself to breathe.

Cary took his mother's hand. "Mom, tell us what's wrong." He followed the woman's stare. "What is it? This is Shannon, the woman I told you about."

Before he turned his attention back to his mother, Shannon saw worry in Cary's eyes. Pat blinked a few times then averted her gaze and Shannon was glad for the reprieve. However, the deep frown that creased the woman's brow did little to boost her confidence.

"I guess I just got faint from hunger. I'm sorry." She took a deep breath. "I'll be fine, really, just give me a minute to sit here." She glanced once again at Shannon. "Honey, forgive my manners. Welcome to our home."

"Thank you. I'm sorry you're not feeling well."

Cary stood and she longed to take his hand for moral support, but she didn't have to, he took hers. She wondered what was going through his mother's mind each time she looked at him then back at Shannon, as if she knew something they didn't.

"You two make a handsome couple indeed. I knew the right woman would find my son one day. I believe that day is here."

"Mom, please, we hardly know each other."

Pat smiled. "Yes, but you feel like you've known each other for a lifetime. Am I right?"

"How could you know that?"

"Ah, mothers recognize these things, dear."

Shannon gazed into Cary's eyes and the charge that usually passed between them was stronger than ever. She remembered Cary's words from that afternoon. Could he be right? Was what was happening between them something that was beyond their control?

Hayley cleared her throat and broke the hex that bound her brother and Shannon. "Well, shall we eat before mother has another spell, or her intuition tells us more than we want to know?"

Cary put his car in gear and drove through the

gate toward the highway. He glanced over at Shannon and saw the confused look on her face. "Penny for your thoughts."

"Oh, I was just thinking about the things your mom said this evening."

"Do you think she's crazy?"

"No, don't talk like that. It's just—"

"Just what?" He took her hand and rubbed his thumb across its softness. Her skin was like satin under his touch. He longed to take her in his arms and protect her from what was bothering her. However, he knew what was on her mind. It had been on his all evening.

"Do you remember what you said today at Revamped?"

"About things being beyond our control?" He remembered it well and felt it in his gut. Something was pushing them together.

"Yes."

He momentarily met her gaze, then turned his attention back to the road. She was so beautiful it took his breath away. His whole being was filled with her.

"What if you're right? I mean, I sence it, here." She pointed to her heart. "I've never felt these emotions before, and the strange electricity that passes between us."

They couldn't have this conversation while going down the road. There was a scenic point just around the next curve. He wanted to look into her eyes while they talked. This could be the most important discussion of their lives.

* * *

Shannon was pleased Cary had pulled off the road. She was afraid of what might come to pass between them. Not that she was scared they would actually fall in love, but that they wouldn't. Maybe her feelings were just lust, not love at all.

The thought chilled her to the bone. Never in her wildest dreams did she think that in six weeks' time, she'd meet the man of her dreams, fall in love and feel like their affections had always been.

Cary put the car in park and turned off the headlamps. The parking lights were still on which allowed the dim glow of the instruments in the dash to illuminate the car's interior. She studied his features in the soft light. He was so good-looking it made her ache for his touch, but that wasn't all that attracted her. It was his heart, his eyes, his whole being, that filled her with want. He turned toward her and her hands felt tiny in his grasp.

"I don't know where to start," he said. "All of my life I've been drawn to the Rhea building. I've been fascinated with it and I know almost every nook and cranny of it." He smiled. "Matter of fact, I was about to make an offer on it, but you got there first."

"I'm sorry. Didn't Hayley know you wanted it?"

"No, I never said anything to anyone. I only made the decision the day before you looked at it. And don't be sorry, I think you love that old building almost as much as I do."

"I do love it, very much." She loved him, too,

but those words wouldn't come so easily even though she wanted to blurt them out. His smile warmed her heart and she saw sincerity in his eyes.

"The minute I walked in today, I knew the right person owned the property. Everything is as it should be inside, just as I remember it."

The faraway look in his eyes reminded her of what had happened to her when the feeling of déjà vu overwhelmed her. "Remembered it from when?" When he was a boy? When they were married? This was a ridiculous conversation, she didn't believe in any of it. However, she couldn't deny the emotions that had reeled through her since she'd been in Jonesville Township.

"Well, I'm not quite sure. It's almost like it was in another lifetime."

A cold chill ran up her spine and she couldn't stop the shiver as it made its way to the surface. She turned and faced forward. "May we go please?"

"Why? We need to talk about this."

Now anger began to seep into her mind, or was it fear. Fear of glancing to the unknown. She'd let all the talk about hauntings and ghosts get to her. No, she would not stand for these silly thoughts to occupy her psyche any longer "Really? Talk about what Cary?"

"Us and what's happening between us."

She met his gaze once again, but this time she tried to keep her emotions in check. "What's happening between us is we're attracted to each other. You're a man, I'm a woman. It happens all the time." Did she really believe that?

"Being attracted to someone has never affected

me like this. Has it you? Have you ever experienced the feelings we get when we touch, the static in the air when we're together inside the Rhea building? Haven't you wondered why we feel like we've been there before?"

She had never told him any of these things. "How do you know I feel the same things?"

"Sweetheart, don't try to fool me. I know you like the back of my hand. See, that's what I'm talking about. Why would I say that? Unless—"
Now she was really starting to get uncomfortable with all of this. "Unless, what? We were re-incarnated as someone from the past destined to be together no matter what? That's just stupid, Cary." She couldn't handle any more of this nonsense, but she couldn't deny the feelings she had either. "Take me home, please. I don't want to talk about this or think about it for one more minute."

CHAPTER 7

*Y*ou could have cut the tension in the air with a knife for the rest of the ride back, and she hated it. Why was she being like this? She loved this man and now she was pushing him away.

Cary pulled to the back of the Rhea building and she stepped out of the car. Glad to be back in the fresh air she inhaled a deep breath.

She felt as if Cary's gaze burned into her backside as he followed her up the stairs. "You don't have to walk me to the door; I'm perfectly capable of getting inside myself."

Why the hell hadn't she remembered to turn the porch light on? She fumbled through her purse for her keys, relieved when she touched their cold metal. The light of the moon was just enough to let her put the door key in the lock.

"Shannon, please."

She opened the door and stepped inside. When he tried to follow, she placed her hand against his chest. She couldn't refute the volt of energy that coursed through her, but she chose to ignore it. "Conversation over, Cary. I don't believe in ghosts, reincarnation or hauntings. I never have and never will. I will admit there have been some strange coincidences, but that's just what they are, coincidence."

"But—"

"I'm tired and I'd like to go to bed." She looked into his beautiful green eyes. The sadness she saw in them all but broke her heart. Why couldn't they have just had a normal relationship like other people? She couldn't let this go on. The words all but stuck in her throat, and she fought to get them out. "Please, don't come by for a while. I need to get my thoughts together."

"Don't turn me away like this. We're bound to be together."

"Just give me some space, please."

* * *

Nothing in Cary's life had been so hard as to leave Shannon, get back in his car and drive home. He couldn't understand why she was being so closed minded about their relationship. Yes, it was farfetched and he had never believed in anything like this before, but damnit, his feelings were too strong.

It had been only minutes since he'd dropped her off, but to him it seemed like hours, even days. He didn't want to be away from her for a moment, but she'd made it clear she wanted her space. He was a man of his word, so he'd give it to her.

His mother had acted so strange all evening. It baffled him how she knew the things she did. He was going to find out just exactly why she kept staring at him and Shannon throughout the whole meal.

He closed the gate, got back in his car and pulled into the garage. The attic ladder was down and light shown from the opening to the garage floor. It had been years since he'd been up there.

Reaching the foot of the ladder, he looked up. "Mom, are you up there?"

"No, Cary it's me. She asked me to get this old trunk that's up here, but I can't lift it. Would you help me?"

Why would his mother want Hayley to get a trunk from the attic this time of evening? "Sure."

Cary pulled the oversized suitcase to the edge of the ladder. "I'll go down and you slide it over the side. I'll grab it and take it inside."

It was heavier than he thought, but he managed to get it to the ground without much trouble. "Did she say what this is all about?"

Hayley opened the door leading into the house. "All she said was there was something we needed to know and she didn't think it could wait any longer."

"This was dad's army trunk."

"I know," Hayley replied. "I remember when we used to go through it and look at his old pictures. That was a lifetime ago and before he put this lock on it."

At the mention of 'a lifetime', his thoughts went back to Shannon. "Shannon was freaked out by the night's events. She doesn't want to see me for a while. Said she needs time to get her thoughts together."

"Can you blame her? After what Mom said and the way she stared at the two of you all night, it made me want to crawl under the table."

"I guess it did Shannon, too." He glanced down at the battered green trunk. "We'd better get this inside and find out what this is all about."

Cary's mother sat in her favorite chair, the key to the trunk rested between her fingers. "Mom, are you okay? We don't have to do this tonight. It can wait till tomorrow." Tears welled in her faded green eyes and he realized for the first time that she looked tired.

"No, son, it can't wait." She bent and placed the key in the lock.

The clank of the metal latch hitting the side of the trunk echoed in the quiet of the house. He watched as Pat slowly and carefully opened the lid. Inside his father's dress green lay right on top. His mother began to talk.

"You kids know how much I loved your father, don't you?"

He and Hayley both answered with a nod. His mother and father's love for each other had been evident all of his life. Their love was true and that's what he had hoped to find.

"Cary, I know how much you've always loved that old Rhea building. It's in your blood. Your father and I have known it for a long time."

"Yes, but what does that have to do with Dad's army things."

"Now, don't hurry me. It's taken me a long time to tell you this." She sat back and folded her hands in her lap.

Watching the thoughtful look on his mother's face made Cary even more curious. It was all he could do not to prompt her to continue.

"You know, you might be right." Pat leaned forward and placed the lock back on the trunk.

Now he was more confused than ever. "Right about what?"

"This can wait until tomorrow. I've been keeping this secret a long time. One more day isn't going to matter." She stood and put the key into her pocket. "When the young woman opens tomorrow after lunch, we will take the trunk to town, to the Rhea building. Shannon should hear this, too."

"That won't work, Mom." Cary took a seat on the couch. He would like nothing more than to see Shannon again.

"Of course it will work, darling."

"She doesn't want to see me for a while. After tonight she's confused and," he paused and his heart skipped a beat. He knew what was wrong with her. "And, frightened." He glanced up in time to see his mother smile in understanding.

Pat touched Cary's hand. "Of course she's frightened. Most people are scared of what they don't understand, and some want to deny the existence of the inevitable."

Somehow, he knew exactly what her words meant. However, he'd never seen her act this way before and his mother's mental state worried him. Hayley's voice drew his attention and her words told him she felt the same way.

"Mom, are you sure you're feeling alright?"

The older woman nodded her head. "I feel fine, dear. Tomorrow it will all be clear to everyone and I'll feel even better after that." She turned and walked down the hallway. "Goodnight, my precious children."

Cary looked at his sister and she shrugged. He then glanced at the trunk. What could its contents hold that would bring all of these strange happenings together? One thing he knew for sure, Shannon was not going to be happy when she saw them walk through the door of Revamped.

* * *

Shannon glanced at her watch. One o'clock, time to open the shop. She stepped to the door and turned the lock. The beautiful Sunday afternoon prompted her to prop the door open. The fresh air would do her good after the sleepless night she'd had.

She couldn't get Cary, and everything that had happened, off her mind. The things he'd said, even if she didn't want to face the reality, actually hit home. However, instead of making things clearer, it put questions in her mind.

Why had she been drawn here? She'd never heard of Jonesville Township, but when she looked at the area map for a small town to move to, the name immediately drew her attention. Now that she thought about it, the name all but popped out and hit her in the face.

Damn, why hadn't she realized before now she hadn't even considered looking anywhere else? Also, why did she fall in love with this building only to find out it was called the Rhea Building?

She hadn't thought Rhea was that common of a name. Could it have been an unknown force that drew her here? And what about the immediate feelings she had for Cary. There was love at first sight, at least she'd heard of it, but this was off the charts!

It all made her doubt her own beliefs. Her mother had believed in the supernatural, but her father had always instilled logic and the supernatural wasn't logical. Was it? No. So why did everything point to – "Oh, stop it!" Her mind told her none of it could be true, but her heart told her she and Cary were destined to be together.

A car door closed outside and voices filtered in. She glanced up and saw the man of her dreams. She had told him she didn't want to see him, but he hadn't listened. With each fiber of her body, she wanted to be angry, but as soon as she saw him, all that melted away.

She watched him open the trunk of his car and retrieve an old army box. Her breath caught in her throat. He looked so strong, handsome, and so damn sexy it made her yearn to be in his arms. Why did every emotion she had surface when she saw the man?

Surely the visit was business. Why else would Hayley and Pat have come along? Did they want to display something in her shop, maybe something in the trunk? She took a deep breath in through her nose, and released it slowly out her mouth. It didn't help, her heart still beat wildly. "Focus." Yes, she would force herself to keep her focus on business and not on Cary.

Why was she trying to lie to herself? Business was the last thing on her mind. Seeing Cary, even though she tried to convince herself otherwise, was first and foremost.

A warm breeze rushed through the door just before Cary entered with the old trunk. Dane jingled as if sending out a welcome greeting. It was the breeze that rang the bell, Shannon. The bell didn't ring itself. "Logic," she whispered under her breath.

Cary sat the trunk on the floor beside a small seating area she had for her customer's comfort. He stood to his full height and glanced at her. Embers of passion glowed in his eyes when she met his gaze. The electricity in the air, she'd almost become accustomed to, sparked between them and threatened to steel her breath.

"Shannon. I'm sorry for coming after you asked me not to, but Mother insisted."

She broke the trance he held over her and greeted her guests. "I-it's okay. Hayley, Mrs. Jones, it's good to see you." The warmth of Cary's hand on her shoulder radiated through her body and rested in her heart.

"We need to talk, privately."

It made no sense, but the last, and the first, thing she wanted to do was be alone with this man. She glanced up at him trying not to focus on his green eyes. "Now? It looks like your mom has business we should take care of."

"Now, please."

The look in his eye told her something was very important to him. "Okay, let's go to the store room."

They walked side by side and she remembered the first time she ever saw him. He came out of the very room they were about to enter. She flipped on the light switch and turned toward him. "Is something wrong?"

If she had wanted to protest his kiss, she wouldn't have had time. His lips were warm and inviting on hers and she leaned into him. She knew at that moment she would be with Cary Jones forever. It was meant to be, one way or the other, and she was tired of fighting the truth. She was his forever, mind, body and soul.

He released her lips but held her close. She placed her arms around his waist and snuggled against him. Safe and loved is how she felt. His chest vibrated and tickled her ear when he spoke.

"I had to do that. I missed the hell out of you. I know you didn't want to see me again for a while, but—"

"Shut up. I'm glad you're here." When he chuckled she couldn't help but smile. God she loved him.

"You are?"

She leaned back and gazed into the eyes she'd come to know so well. "Yes, I couldn't stop thinking about you last night, and when I saw you out front I wanted to run away and at the same time, run into your arms."

"I thought of you all night, too. I love you,

Shannon. That's all I know that's real about the chain of events over the last few months. I have fallen in love with you."

The three words she never thought would mean anything again, now meant the world to her. "I love you, too." Had she really pronounced her love? Yes, and it felt great! "I love you. I love you! There, I said it. Out loud and everything, now are you happy?" His smile caused butterflies to flit through her.

"The happiest man in the world."

Her heart sank when his eyes grew serious. She knew he was going to get to the real reason he'd wanted to talk to her in private.

Cary cleared his throat, dropped his arms and took Shannon's hands in his. "I don't know what's in that trunk out there, but whatever it is, my mother thought it important enough for us to be together to see it."

"Where did it come from?"

"It was my dad's. It's been in the attic. He put a lock on it a few years before he died. I never knew why, but I have a feeling we're fixing to find out."

"Then I guess we'd better get back to your mom and Hayley before customers start to come in." She turned toward the door leading into the shop.

"Shannon?"

Stopping at the sound of Cary's voice, she didn't face him. "Yes." His arms encircled her from behind, and she placed her hands on his welcoming his embrace.

"No matter what happens, we are here for each

other, we can't forget that. Right?"

Swallowing the lump in her throat, she nodded, frightened to learn what was in the container, but excited at the same time. At the moment she felt like a living oxymoron, frightened yet excited, torn from one thing to another, yet there was nothing she could do about it. Somehow she knew the love she and Cary had professed to each other wasn't the only thing about to make her life change forever.

CHAPTER 8

Cary sat next to the woman he loved on the small, antique loveseat across from his mother. His mother's hand trembled when she placed the key into the old lock on the trunk.

He was glad Shannon decided to temporarily close Revamped. Especially after his mother said she only wanted a few people to know about what she was going to reveal. The older woman took a deep breath as if to calm herself and he felt sorry for her.

Pat Jones had always been there for him, so he knew whatever she held secret would be hard for her to reveal.

"Cary, Hayley, when your father passed away two years ago, you know how much I missed him." Tears twinkled in her eyes as she removed the lock and unlatched the case. "I still do, but I want you to know, I knew nothing about the things I'm about to show you."

She pulled a piece of paper from her pocket. "I have to read this to you then we'll go on to the belongings of the trunk. I found this note in some of your dad's things along with the key to this lock, and another key."

Cary watched as his mother placed a very old looking key on the table. He then saw Hayley shift in her chair as if she knew what the key went to. Shannon reached over and picked up the small metal object.

Turning it over in her hand, she studied it. "Mrs. Jones, I think this key goes to the lock on the antique glass cabinet over there that belonged to the Rheas."

Hayley nodded her head. "That's what I thought, Shannon."

"You girls are right, that's precisely the lock it opens." Pat unfolded the paper in her hand.

Frowning Hayley said, "But I thought there was only one key to that lock."

"Let me read this. It will explain a lot." Pat placed her glasses on her nose.

"My beautiful wife, I know you've found the keys. Let me explain. First, of all you are the love of my life. You have stood at my side through thick and thin, but if you're reading this, now you stand alone.

This isn't going to be easy, my love, but it's something I had to do for our family. You and I have both wondered for years if Cary was Clifford Rhea, reincarnated."

Shannon's gasp tore Cary's attention from his mother. Had he heard the woman right? They thought he was Clifford? He put his arm around Shannon's shoulder. "Mom, don't--"

Pat held up her hand. "Now, Cary, let me finish before you jump to conclusions. Please?"

He felt Shannon tremble beneath his embrace and pulled her tighter. "Shannon?"

She leaned into him. "I want to hear it all. Get this out in the open so it can be over with."

Pat nodded and continued, "In the wedding picture we have of the Rhea's, Clifford bears a striking resemblance to our son, but after in-depth research, I now can tell you why.

You, my dear, are Clifford and Willena's great, great niece. Your great-great grandmother was Clifford Rhea's sister.

Hayley placed her hand over her mother's. "You mean we are ancestors of the Rheas, Mom?"

Patting her daughter's hand, Pat said, "That's right, honey, we are."

"How exciting! I knew there was something about those people I loved, Now I know why. We're kin to them."

The sparkle in Cary's sister's eyes showed real happiness. However, he didn't know how to take the news. How long had his father known? "Mom, why didn't dad tell us about this?"

His mother looked down at the hand she held the paper in, and with her free hand, twisted the wedding band she still wore. "There's a lot more to it than a simple explanation, honey. Your father, God rest his soul, being the town's historian, had access to records that weren't available to the general public. He found some that had been put aside and apparently forgotten.

She held the letter out in front of her and began to read again. "I discovered some old, immigration papers in the courthouse basement. Clifford and Willena and your grandmother's were among them. Cliff's sister's name was Sarah. The documents had been discarded for some odd reason, but I salvaged them and you'll find them in the root cellar under the Rhea building."

"Root cellar?" Cary couldn't believe what he was hearing.

"Yes, honey, and there's a way to get to it from the storeroom of this building."

That was impossible. Cary knew every inch of this old building. He'd surely know if there was a door in the storeroom leading to a root cellar. "I've never seen anything that could lead under the building. Maybe Dad was mistaken."

Shaking her head, Pat said, "No, there's no mistake. Your father found out about the old cellar when he found the drawing that Clifford Rhea had made of how he was going to build this place. It included the cellar and the apartment above."

This was almost too much to take in at one time. He could only imagine how Shannon felt. He glanced at her and she was totally focused on Pat. When Dane chimed out, Cary looked up to see Johnny Franklin enter, then close the door behind him. His father's longtime friend approached without a word.

He met Shannon's gaze. "I thought you locked that door."

"I did, too. I know I put the closed sign up."

Pat smiled at the older man and laid the letter aside. "Perfect timing, John, have a seat."

Cary stood, and reached to shake Johnny's hand. "Good to see you."

"I was rather surprised to get your mother's call this morning." He accepted Cary's handshake then sat in a vacant chair.

Returning to his place beside Shannon, he took her hand and glanced at his mother. "It seems she's full of surprises as of late."

"Yes, well." Pat cleared her throat. "As I told you kids last night, I've been waiting for a good while to get this all out in the open. So, I wanted Johnny to know, too."

"Know what?" Johnny looked at container on the table. "Is that Jones' old trunk?"

Pat nodded. "Yes. Okay, everyone please let me finish."

Listening while his mother filled Johnny in on what she'd been telling them, Cary began to let it all sink in. But there was still so much that didn't make since. Hidden rooms, historical records, immigrants, and they were kin to the Rheas? He only hoped when all was said and done, he'd understand.

"Johnny, my husband dug a tunnel many years ago that is a passageway to the root cellar."

"A passageway, Mother?" Cary could tell by the look on Johnny's face that the man was also having a hard time with all of this.

"Yes, son. According to your father's letter, the owners that bought this building, after my uncle died, didn't want to use the cellar, so they simply closed it up by covering the stairway with floor.

"On one of the occasions when the building was empty, your father cut some of the plank flooring out and made an opening so he could get in and out of the building without anyone's knowledge. That's how he got some of these things." Pat opened the trunk.

Had his father been the one taking items from all of the previous owners over the years? He didn't want to believe that, but all fingers pointed to that very thing.

Cary vowed to find the secret hiding place beneath the building, but now, he wanted to see what was among his father's belongings. On top of the contents lay Cary's dad's army uniform and hat. He'd been through these things a hundred times when he was younger, and that's exactly how he remembered them lying every time. "What things, Mother?"

She pulled out the uniform, put it to her nose and took a deep breath then placed it beside her. Beneath it was an old frame. He imagined it was the Rhea's wedding photo as she lay the frame face down on the uniform.

"All of these things originally belonged to Clifford and Willena Rhea."

Cary sat forward and gazed into the trunk. Trinkets, a beautiful old dress, some pictures and a small wooden box among other things were inside.

Shannon stood and started to reach into the trunk then paused. "May I, Mrs. Jones?"

Pat pushed the trunk closer to her. "Of course."

Her heart raced as she touched the fabric of the

very old, off white dress. It was simple, yet elegant and she fell in love with it immediately. Not knowing how fragile the material might be, she tried to be gentle as she pulled it out. "Isn't this lovely?"

Letting it fall to its full length, she realized what it was. "This is Willena's wedding gown, isn't it?" A smile lifted the corners of Pat Jones' lips.

"Indeed it is. My husband and I bought it, and the Rhea's wedding picture, right after we married. We stopped at a small antique dealer's shop while we were on our honeymoon. Something drew my husband to the items and he wouldn't leave without them. We didn't know until we took the frame off of the picture to look for markings that it was the Rheas. You can imagine how we felt."

"Amazing." The story was wonderful, but it didn't touch the beauty of the garment she held. It was soft, pliable and still had the scent of perfume on it. No, that was only her imagination. "This cloth is over 150 years old and it still looks new! It's been so well preserved." Careful not to let the fabric touch the ground, she folded the dress back the way it was and placed it on the couch where she'd been sitting.

There were so many items in the trunk; she didn't know what to look at next. Then she noticed a small wooden box. It was amongst everything else but it seemed to stand out.

No matter how hard she tried, she couldn't quiet the tremble of her hand when she reached for the box. She realized Cary now stood beside her and when he placed his arm around her waist, calm swept over her and the trembling subsided.

"Want me to get it?"

His voice soothed her even further. Every emotion she'd ever felt, again ran rampant through her. It had to be the anticipation of having these treasures in front of her.

She wasn't sure what rested inside the little package, but in her heart, she knew it was something precious. She swallowed the lump in her throat and nodded her head. Cary reached into his father's trunk and carefully picked up the box. Shannon paid attention when Pat began to read again.

"There are other items in the root cellar as well.

"When you read this, you will know who has been taking the items from the Rhea building all of these years. I couldn't stand to see these historical things leave our little community, and when we were younger, you and I could have never afforded to buy them all. Please, forgive me.

"Please tell my son and daughter I love them very much and now that they know the secret, I hope they can forgive me, too.

"Pat, I hated lying to you, but you would have tried to stop me, and I felt compelled to continue."

Shannon listened in stunned silence to Ben Jones' words. The man had been the one that had stolen the items. The look on Cary's face told her it was something he never thought his dad would do, but the truth lay in front of him, and there was more beneath the building. Her heart went out to the man she loved.

Pat wiped a tear from her cheek reached into

the bottom of the trunk and pulled out a manila envelope. She continued to read, "However, you will find money, the names, phone numbers and addresses of everyone who owned the things I took. There should be enough to pay for each item. Then these treasures will truly belong to you and the kids to do with what you want.

"The key to the lock on the Rhea's cabinet is in there as well. I had it made many years ago. That's how I gained access to the case."

"Here, Cary, I can't read anymore. I've read it a hundred times and know it by heart."

He took the paper from his mother and read the rest to himself. Hayley and John comforted Pat while Shannon reached for the picture that still lay face down on the uniform. Pat touched her hand and she met the older woman's gaze.

"Are you sure you're ready to look at that?"

Of course she wanted to look at it. Why would Pat even ask such a thing? She nodded and Pat released her grasp, picked up the photo and handed it to her.

Her breath caught in her throat when she saw the faded image. It couldn't be. Her knees were going to buckle beneath her. Cary's voice calling her name echoed in the distance and the world around her faded to black.

* * *

Damp coolness washed over Shannon's face and neck. She felt comfortable and safe, but what had happened? The ringing in her ears quieted and she heard a man and woman talking. Everything became clearer and she was suddenly in reality.

"Shannon? Shannon?"

Cary's voice was filled with concern and when she opened her eyes he was sitting on the edge of the bed. Her own bed and Cary wiped her face with a wet cloth while Hayley stood behind him and gazed at her with worried eyes.

She forced the words out but wasn't sure she wanted to know. "What happened? How did I get up stairs?"

Cary bent and kissed her. Gentle, caring, yet passionate and she welcomed it. Then she heard Hayley clear her throat.

"Ummm... welcome back."

Cary released her lips, straightened and met her gaze. "I carried you up here after you fainted when you saw the photo of Clifford and Willena."

The memory came flooding back. "Oh, my gosh! It's us, Cary. That's us in that picture." Could it be they were really the Rheas reincarnated? It went against every logical thing her father had instilled in her, however she couldn't help but wonder.

A shiver ran up her spine. Had she lived before? Is that why she fell in love with Cary instantly? She couldn't bring herself to look away from his green eyes. The man she loved reassured her with his smile.

"I admit, at first glance, the resemblance is uncanny, but you have to remember that Clifford's blood runs in my veins. I do look like him, but that's not me in that picture." He handed her the photo.

She was almost afraid to look at it again, but she forced herself. Amazed at the resemblance between Clifford and Cary, she now saw the differences. However, she was even more astounded at her likeness to Willena. "That's all well and good but what about—"

"You looking like Willie? I don't know, but we might find the answer in the documents in the cellar."

Hayley stepped forward. "Speaking of the cellar, and now that I know you're okay, I'm going to go see what Mom and John have found down there."

EPILOGUE

$\mathcal{S}$hannon glanced at the engagement ring on her finger. Soon it would be coupled with Willena's gold wedding band and she and Cary would be married.

"Only five minutes before you walk down the aisle and become my sister-in-law." Hayley straightened Shannon's veil.

"Shannon," Pat said, "You look stunning in that dress. Willena would be proud to know you are wearing it. Such a perfect fit."

It was a perfect fit and this was a perfect day, the day she would become the man of her dreams' wife. She felt really beautiful for the first time in her life. "Thank you."

"Not only does it look spectacular on you, but it will go perfect on the manikin in the new museum." Pat dabbed at her eyes with a tissue. "I only wish Ben was here to see all of this."

Hayley put her arm around her mother's

shoulder. "He would be pleased at the way things panned out."

Shannon was ecstatic that she and Cary made the decision to turn the Rhea building into the Rhea Museum. She still couldn't believe none of the previous owners would take any money for the items that had belonged to them, but instead, donated it all to the Museum.

Even though she owned the Rhea building, she didn't feel she had the right to any of the things in the trunk, or what they found in the cellar. The only things they kept were the Rheas wedding rings. Her heart soared when the Crawford's insisted on it; after all they bought the rings originally and were the rightful owners so she graciously accepted.

The empty wooden box that once held the precious gold would sit in the original Rhea's cabinet. She had a plaque made stating gratitude and thanks to the couple for their gift. Hayley's voice pulled her from her thoughts.

"I'm just glad we found out you're not our long lost cousin or something."

"Me, too. If that would have been the case, I wouldn't be marrying your brother today and you wouldn't be my maid of honor."

They'd done hours of research and found it was simply coincidental that her late husband's name was Rhea and that she resembled Willena. Thanks to her dad's teachings, she'd stayed grounded through everything that had happened. She knew there had to be logical explanations.

Well, for everything except Dane. He rang more merrily then ever these days. Maybe it just seemed that way because she was so happy. The world was brighter and the weight of her previous life was lifted from her shoulders, never to return.

The door opened and Cassie Franklin entered with a grin. "It's time, ladies." She approached Pat. "Mrs. Jones, Papa John's waiting to walk you down the aisle and get you seated, then he'll join Cary at the front of the church. Hayley, you go next to take your place at the front across from Papa John."

The young lady had helped so much in the planning of the wedding and had taken control of the food. Franklin's was catering the reception, and Shannon was impressed at how organized Cassie was. Shannon saw a sweet smile cross Cassie's face.

"Cary's waiting for you, Miss Shannon. Are you ready?"

She was more ready than she ever thought possible. She followed the others then stood in the doorway leading into the small chapel.

Her heart wouldn't stop pounding. Within the next few minutes she would be Mrs. Cary Jones. She never thought she'd find true love, but she couldn't deny it had happened.

Looking up, she met his gaze. His mesmerizing green eyes took her to another place and everything around her disappeared. At that moment, she felt as if only she and Cary existed in the world, her world, no, their world.

He was the most handsome man she'd ever seen. Standing tall and proud, he winked at her. That's all it took for her knees to become weak. The pure excitement of knowing she'd be in his arms in a few short hours released an abundance of butterflies in her stomach. Heat rose to her cheeks in anticipation of what the night would hold.

"Shannon."

Cassie's whisper drew her from her private thoughts and she realized the wedding march was playing. She stepped into the chapel and walked down the aisle toward her man. His smile warmed her heart and the twinkle in his eye said he looked forward to their wedding night, too.

The pastor's words all but faded into the distance as she concentrated on the love of her life. He was everything she'd ever wanted.

Something had drawn her to this little town, to Cary Jones. Everything proved to be logical, but she couldn't deny there was at least something a little mystical about their love. Whatever it was, she wouldn't question it.

"The rings, please." The pastor took the rings from John. "These golden bands represent the eternal circle of love. They are special in more ways than one but now they will forever belong to Shannon and Cary." He handed Shannon one of the bands. "Place this on Cary's finger and repeat after me."

Her voice came out barely above a whisper. She didn't care, the only one who needed to hear her was Cary. Tears welled in his eyes as she repeated the sacred vows and pushed the ring into place.

The preacher gave Cary the remaining band. "Cary, place this on Shannon's finger and repeat after me."

Cary took her left hand in his and placed the golden ring, which represented his eternal love, on her finger. She closed her eyes as a tear slid down her cheek. She loved this man far beyond anything she could have imagined.

"You may kiss the bride."

Applause broke out and echoed through the room when Cary took her mouth with his. When his lips left hers he held her tight. His breathy whisper was warm, but his words sent a shiver of delight down her spine.

"Our lives have been...revamped."

SPRINGTIME SNOW

Judith Cane sat at her desk and stared at the document on the laptop screen in front of her. The page silently glared back with only two words typed in the center, CHAPTER 15.

It had been three days since she'd written a single word. Frustration settled in, tears threatened to spill onto her cheek and she began to type the first thing that came to mind. Being a published romance author is totally over rated! Then she slammed the computer shut, stood and went to her favorite chair.

The fire blazing in the hearth heated the room, but did nothing to warm her chilly mood. "Boy, Charlie, I'm in a foul frame of mind today aren't I?" Today and every day, it seemed as of late. She bent and patted the canine atop the head then sat down and pulled a throw over her legs. "Tell me, how's a woman supposed to write a story about love and romance when her life is totally void of it?"

She couldn't help but smile when the old dog whined his protest. "I know you love me fella. I love you, too, but I'm talking about love of the human kind. Man being the three key letters in that word." Having Charlie there helped relieve some of her stress and she was grateful for that.

Grey clouds drifted across the sky above the Ozarks. The first day of spring had come over a week ago and that was just about how long it had been since she'd been out of the house. She swore if it snowed one more inch, she would absolutely scream.

She studied Charlie all cuddled up on his bed next to the fireplace. "You know what buddy? Springtime's supposed to bring Lilacs, Black-eyed Susan's, Honeysuckle and green grass. Not snow." Man, she sounded like a pouting teenager. What was happening to her?

Her mind wandered back to her wedding day. At one time she'd loved Zachary Cane more than life itself. He'd been a great husband at first, then jealousy plagued him. So what if she made more money writing than he did as a bank executive. It didn't matter to her, she loved him.

However, it bothered him. He started drinking then lost his job, and took it out on her. He'd said it was her fault that his life was going to hell. It wasn't, she knew it and refused to let him take her down with him.

The memories of good times and bad tugged at her heart. No wonder she was depressed. The only man she would ever love, or ever wanted to love, let the whisky bottle take over his life. She couldn't compete with that.

Judith glanced around the beautiful room that surrounded her. She had once enjoyed being there with her husband, but at this point in time she wished Zach had the place stuck snugly up his nose.

The dog suddenly started to bark. Bang, clank! "What in the...?" Noises from outside penetrated the quiet of the evening. Clatter...crash!

Glancing out of the huge bay window of the living room she saw the solid white yard and driveway, but nothing else. Had a car crashed? "I have to hurry, Charlie, someone might be hurt."

Her coat went on easily then she pulled on her boots, opened the front door and rushed onto the porch. Thankfully she'd shoveled snow from the walk the day before but beyond that it was a couple foot deep. Looking up at the sky, she realized it was almost dust. "We'd better get a flashlight, boy." Charlie panted with excitement as he followed her.

Back inside she checked the flashlight batteries. On her way back out she retrieved her cell phone from the kitchen counter. She didn't get great reception in the house, but from the main road she could call 911 if she needed to.

Charlie leaped over the snow toward the highway. Through the naked trees of winter, the faint glow of headlights moved slowly up her drive. "Charlie, come back here." Whoever had crashed must have been okay. At least the car was still drivable. But why wouldn't they go back to town instead of coming toward her house?

Realty struck and she realized her vulnerability. Taking a deep breath, she tried to slow her racing pulse. She had to get back to the house, quickly. "Charlie, come here." The canine hesitated then followed obediently.

At least she had her pepper spray for protection. A lump formed in her throat when she entered the house, then shut and locked the door. She was afraid. For the first time, she was scared of being alone.

The portable land line phone felt cool when she picked it up on the way to the bay window. After closing the blinds she peeked out at the car that, little by little, approached the house.

She dropped the blind slat back into place, stepped away and placed her hand to her throat. Closing her eyes, she took a deep breath. She couldn't have a panic attack, not right now, she needed to stay calm. It could mean the difference between life and death. "Come on, Judith, get it together."

Charlie's tail wagged as if nothing was wrong. Why hadn't she had the Labrador trained to be a guard dog? He'd be useless against an intruder.

The sound of the car motor came to an abrupt stop just outside the house. She ran into the bedroom, grabbed her pepper spray then hurried back to the window to look out.

The shadowed shape of a man got out of the car, but the dim light of dusk made it impossible to see the figure clearly. She thought she would stop breathing completely when she recognized the man who approached her door. "Zach?" What was he doing there? He was drunk. He had to be.

Fear turned to anger as she heard him stomp the

snow from his feet at the front door. How dare he invade her privacy in his drunkenness?

"Charlie, stop wagging your tale. He's not going to be here long, so don't act like you're happy to see him. You hear me." Little good her scolding did. Her supposed best friend ignored her. "Fine."

She went to the door and jerked it open before Zach could ring the doorbell. She glared at him. His eyes were bright and his six foot two frame stood tall and steady. Was he sober? No, she didn't dare have hope of that.

Locking the glass outer door between them she asked, "What do you want, Zach? This is my house now. You have no right to be here." His smile dazzled her, as it had in years past and his deep voice penetrated her very soul. How she missed his arms around her, his gentle kiss everything about the way he was in the beginning.

"Baby, I want to talk to you. Please, let me in."

Baby, he hadn't called her that since months before the divorce was final. "Go back to town, get a motel and sleep it off."

"I don't need to sleep anything off, Jude. I'm sober, I swear."

The same old lie. Would he ever give up? "If you're sober why'd you run into something on the main road trying to pull in?"

"Helloooo...There's two foot of snow on the ground and the grader hasn't been buy." He leaned against the door frame. "Once I lost you, Jude, I knew I'd thrown away the best thing that had ever happened to me. I wanted to make sure I could stay sober before I tried to get you back. Baby, I've been sober for almost a year now."

She didn't want to listen, but he was saying everything she'd dreamed of hearing since they'd separated. "How can I believe you?"

"Let me in, smell my breath. I promise. It's true. I even got my job back. They gave me a leave of absence for six weeks. I told them how much I love you and that I had to have you back."

Did she dare trust him? Her mind screamed no, but her heart cried yes. Yes! Cautiously she reached for the lock, released it and stood back while Charlie greeted the man he'd known all of his life.

When Zach met her gaze, she almost lost her breath. He looked wonderful. Strong, handsome and…sober. The warmth of his arms penetrated the heavy coat she wore and his breath was a whisper on her lips.

"See? No whisky breath."

His mouth took hers in a passionate kiss and she melted into his embrace. She fought the urge to protest when he released her. His dark brown eyes were indeed clear and his mouth sweet with his unique taste.

"I'm sorry, sweetheart, for the heartache I've caused you. If you'll give me a second chance, I'll prove I can be the best husband you could ever want."

* * *

"Now this is what I'm talking about, Charlie." Judith smiled and let the sun warm her face as she edited the last page of her novel. "Springtime in the Ozarks, you can't beat it, old buddy." Zach's arms came around her from behind the porch swing. His warm breath made her shiver with delight when he whispered in her ear.

"You can't beat falling in love all over again either."

It was true. It had been a month since he'd crashed into the mailbox and shown up on her door step. One glorious springtime month filled with love, sobriety and writing.

ABOUT THE AUTHOR

Hi,

Thank you for taking time to finish this collection of short stories. I hope you enjoyed them. I am in the process of writing more. Look for them in upcoming volumes.

Let me tell you a little about myself. I live in the beautiful Ozarks with my husband and two Cocker Spaniels, Dude and Lacy. I have seventeen grandkids and two great grands... that's right, I'm too young, I know... =) But I love each and every one of them with all my heart and wouldn't change a thing.

My husband and I are retired road musicians. We have a boutique recording studio in our home and record everything from karaoke to live bands.

We've been together thirty wonderful years and still like each other. Go figure.

We are working on getting my stories out in audio format. That's so much fun to do. If you go to YouTube and type in my name, you can hear me sing and also listen to a short audio story I wrote and narrated. It's not really romance, more like paranormal, but I think you'll like it. It's called *House of Silence*

I became interested in writing romance in the early 1990's. A friend suggested we write a book together, so I took her up on it. It opened a whole new world for me. I absolutely love writing, editing, and teaching the basics of writing to others.

Affordable Creative Editing Service is another business I'm involved in. My partner Kathy and I call it ACES. The two of us teach classes, critique and edit fiction books of all genres. http://www.affordablecreativeediting.com is our web address if you know anyone who might want to use our expertise. We've even edited for romance author Lori Copeland. I love her stories.

Well, once again, thank you so much for reading my stories. Please feel free to email me at skizholmes@ymail.com with comments.

I'm looking forward to hearing from you!
Sharon

pass it along

Sheree -

28496272R00109

Made in the USA
Charleston, SC
14 April 2014